TAKEN DEAD

IFE . CHUKWU . DE

PROLOGUE: JULY WEDDING

Ójó ijo-meta as it's described in Yoruba; the rains had been on for three days without letting, a phenomenon also referred to asor mmiriózó ubosi-ato in Igbo language.

Most parts of Lagos were half under water, other parts were just muddy and traffic was at a frustrating stand-still because of the potholes and roads submerged under floodwater. Yet, for the little children it was a welcome experience in the summer heat as they could play soccer all day in the rain and not break a sweat. One adults poison was indeed a child's food.

Somewhere in one of the housing estates in Isolo; downstairs of a four-story block of flats - a big cauldron was on the fire; a decorated "dowry" he-goat was tethered nearby while the women worked feverishly and hastily in a bid to catch the ceremony upstairs on the third floor. It was like a scaled down boat regatta and the goat bleated as if scolding them to get going faster, somewhat oblivious of his not so pleasant future, then again maybe it was well aware of the impending doom and was screaming for mercy or some savior to come to its rescue!

Upstairs people were gathered round in the parlor very ceremoniously yet without a sense of urgency, at first it looked like a council of war or dispute settling occasion. It was supposed to be a "dowry" discussion and payment meeting which was customary for their part of the country. Usually, the groom's family would make a formal request to have audience with their soon to be in-laws for a negotiation of the dowry amount and rites. a very ostentatious process that a lot of brides and grooms look forward. At first it could be assumed that a person was being sold to another family but, in human eyes and the society you are judged by what you do rather than your intentions. As a wise man once said, "God judges us by our intentions; man, judges by actions".

In some cultures, dowry process can take days to months of trying to demonstrate value of a loved through giving of wealth and possibly bloodletting by wrestling match or some other competition. These days it's all down to the coins. It involves a lot of negotiating as if purchasing an item from the market and in most cases professional negotiators are recommended for high class families. In some cultures, after the intense negotiations, only gifts to relatives are accepted or gifts to the bride, while the parents tend to return the dowry back to the in-laws as a declaration that their ward is handed in trust and love rather than sold or bought. In summary it is more ceremonial than transactional, it should be after all it is a celebration of love.

The bride's family was well represented likewise the groom's, as is the custom the bride had to stay out of sight; for this particular ceremony the only difference was that the groom was not physically present as he was out of the country working in one of the oil rich Mediterranean countries; his cousin, Desmond Kobimdi had to stand in for him.

Desmond was a friend to the bride as they had been schoolmates, also the other family members had agreed to this since he was the next in age to the groom as well as a consolidation gesture of the family ties; most importantly the groom could not travel out of the country where he was working as his immigration documents were not regularized yet and any attempt to cross borders would only cause him and his employers' untold hardship! That was how Desmond at twenty and a secondary school leaver got involved in someone else's marriage.

The bride's family, as part of the dowry had asked for fifteen thousand naira for the "bride price" and on this faithful day the groom's family had come to negotiate everything down. Fifteen thousand naira could buy a brand-new Peugeot 504 car with some money left in one's pocket to start up a good business. Most of the items demanded for, according to the traditional eastern marriage requirements (actually a six-page type-written list) had been presented.

Suddenly one of the women from the bride's side, representing their women associations stood up, interrupting the proceedings to raise dust over the size of "ópórókó (stock-fish)" presented, she said,

"My people, greetings; our in-laws I greet you too but there is something wrong with this ókpórókó, this is not the size we use, it is unacceptable!"

As with all such traditional 'hanging of bag' or "ikóbé akpa" (in Illah) or introduction and dowry discussions, an argument ensued over the Ópórókó".

Briefly tempers flared amongst the women folk while the men; young and old laughed and jeered at the unfolding drama. Someone from the bride's family interjected,

"Don't you our in-laws know this girl has school certificate?" Desmond and his kinsmen chorused in response,

"And don't you know our brother is a graduate!"

Eventually the ópórókó issue was resolved with cash compensation by the groom, while every other requirement was met with minimum criticism, and then came the bride price.

The representative of the bride's family cleared his throat and spoke;

"Greetings our in-laws, greetings our people, the main reason why we are here is with us, our in-laws have impressed us tremendously but they still have a short distance left to go. The bride price stipulated before we give our daughter off to you is the issue now it can be paid at once or by installments, in fact to show how flexible we are about its payment; the father of the bride has not finished paying the wife's dowry, it can be passed onto their children… anyway our family has asked us to communicate this amount to you… each stick represents one thousand naira,"

A plate containing fifteen broomsticks was passed to the groom's family.

After a while the Kobimdi family returned the plate to their in-laws and their spokesman said,

"This is how much we are offering each stick represents one hundred naira; only the broken ones are our offer…."

The bride's spokesman laughed and said,

"My in-laws there are only five broken pieces here, are you deducting that from our offer or what…?"

The groom's side replied,

"Precisely five sticks of our own value only!"

The ópórókó woman stood up fiercely and shouted,

"What kind of joke is this, ehn? Look, this girl had finished her secondary school, and you insult us and this girl's virginity, if you people are not ready then leave our daughter for us!"

One of Desmond's cousins, Uche stood up and shouted her down then continued to speak though no one noticed he'd had too much to drink already, he said,

"what is the big deal about this your daughter that you don't want us to have some peace, this one that we are accepting like a damaged good to marry, and who told you she is a virgin, this girl that Desmond taught how to mind her menstrual cycle, if you don't want our offer then, you can go and will youmarry her yourselves! "

Hissed then sat down without a care. Even though he made the last phew phrases with a drunken slur, the tense atmosphere made it pass unnoticed by the groom's parents.

Suddenly everyone was quiet as the implications of Uche's words dawned on the gathering.

Desmond's father broke the silence by first admonishing Uche, "Uche! You get a splash of alcohol on your skin and you lose all sensibilities and decorum and your tongue starts to dance like a demon splashed with holy water! Common be gone from this place!", then confronting his son;

"Nonso is this true?"

But before he could reply the groom's mother attacked him,

"You are asking him if it is true, eeheeenn! So your son betrayed my son and actually had the audacity to be here, our so called king to be so this is how you and your son will be leading us, abomination; aluuuééé!"

And she threw herself on the floor pulling off her clothes. Desmond was looking confused and scared, the groom's immediate elder brother tried to grab at Desmond but he was restrained by others, who were closest to him,

"You bastard I will kill you, no I will castrate you!"

Desmond attempted;

"Bu-, but, I-I-I, Uche is lying…"

He was cut short;

"Shut up you liar…,"

For a second time, he reached for Desmond. Desmond's father raised his voice and spoke,

"Don't insult my son or you insult me…,"

Before he could finish someone threw their drink at him. What ensued was the chaos of people restraining different individuals so as to avoid an all-out riot and it quickly degenerated to exchange of unpleasant words and exposé of deep-rooted long family animosities. Eventually the riot had become unbearable so Desmond and his parents had to leave the wedding.

The sudden turn of events had left Desmond bewildered and confused; he cried the entire drive back home. His father wasn't sure if his son was guilty or not, he also suspected that the issue was really targeted at him because of the announcement of his being next in line to the throne for their town's traditional ruler, the Ogbéléani.

He had never fancied himself as or aspired to being a traditional ruler in the first place but in the current scheme of things it had become a means to an end- the social status elevation; the opportunity to own land and start his own farm and of course the government would need him to keep his people in check, the concept was quite attractive yet it had placed his family smack in the middle of the tussle that ensued. His mind briefly wandered to that risk but he kept all his thoughts to himself for a later discuss with his pregnant wife.

He had been a successful civil servant who had done certain things in his career to get where he was but by no means terrible, he wasn't a very religious man though, one thing he told himself was

"They could have their crown or staff whatever their sign of office was and no one was going to harm his family". When they were alone he told his wife what he thought; she was always his confidant, she smiled at him and held his head to her stomach speaking softly to him about how she trusted him to make the right decision, how she knew their son did not do any of those things and for a while they were silent listening to the beat of the heart in her womb. She didn't allow her fear to show, though her sigh made her to vibrate all over.

The next morning a delegation from the clan that had been sent to chief Kobimdi arrived at his house. Without mincing words, they told him the purpose of their visit which was to take his son, Desmond back to the village with them to face trial and be fined appropriately for his offences so that the bad blood could be cleansed off.

Desmond's father calmly refused saying,

"So, you come to my house to demand for an innocent boy, my son, to be handed over to you to go and sacrifice to your lifeless and heathen gods, you people seem to have forgotten that I also grew up there! Anyway, I have questioned my son and he is innocent, he is even still a virgin, but we all know that my son's indiscretions are not the real issue at stake here; it is the 'Ogbeleani' throne, eh. Go back and tell my brother that I don't want his throne and he can use the staff to replace his impoverished manhood but my son stays with me in this house, this place, my very own God given kingdom! Safe journey; GUARDS!!! Come and show these people the way out and don't let anyone into this house again today!"

And he left them. The guards saw them off to the gate, though the ethnic barrier prevented them from understanding what the visitors were saying they did not miss the atmosphere of anger.

After they had gone one guard commented to the other,

"Kai, Bala but these people they never came for good…,"

Bala responded. "Walahi did you see the way oga said we should throw them out, Yusuf? I think trouble is in the wind, bring our arrows and swords, somehow this Emirship they want to give Maigida is bringing trouble for him and his household!"

Yusuf answered. "Yowaa! You mean cutting down our enemies like in the old days…, "

" Look son, don't ever look forward to it, yes just like my days at the Bagauda court during the Emirship tussles, Allah have mercy on us all."

Then both sank into silence reminiscing as they worked their weapons. Yusuf had never really seen battle, but the stories he heard as a child filled him with awe and he always wanted to be a warrior like his father. Unfortunately, those stories usually left out the part about its

ugliness, death, harm and that no one really ever won in a war; the collateral damage is always

heavy on both sides and sometimes even the victor suffers more than the vanquished.

At about eleven p.m. same day a Fiat lorry parked opposite the gate of the Kobimdi's compound. From another building a petrol bomb landed just before the stairs simultaneously a shout for Desmond's head!

The noise woke Desmond's father who had become a light sleeper thanks to surviving the last civil war; it never left most of his generation, learning to survive bombing after bombing, sometimes days crawling through the jungle to avoid being captured and executed by government forces. He jumped out of bed, woke his wife and dashed into his wardrobe, brought out a bag and 2 guns. Almost instantly Desmond rushed into their room mumbling,

"Papa! We are under attack by armed robbers!"

His father just handed him a pistol saying,

"Take your mother to her sister's place. And don't look back for anything or anyone, not even me, go now!"

Chief turned to his wife;

"Darling you hold on to the kids and the Will and run, don't look back. I'll try and hold them back for a while then join you later… I promise we'll be together again soon; I'll just go and secure the gate so to prevent them from coming up the stairs…,".

A scream from one of the guards shook them,

" Just run."

He made sure they escaped through the rear window, then he took the front and ran out down the stairs with a machete in one hand and a revolver in the other.

He thought to himself, "I have to prevent them from coming up the stairs to the balcony, I shouldn't have built my house like this. Damn it!"

His mind processing the reality of the situation. He wasn't a man of violence but he had gotten accustomed to violent situations too often in his life. That notwithstanding, he had to prevent the attack from getting into his house. He knew he would probably not make it but so he prayed,

"Please God spare my wife and kids."

He made a sign of the Cross.

Noticing one of his guards was down in the pool of his own blood, his stomach twisted. It was difficult to make out which one of them it was. He knew it was serious; the mob wasn't there to threaten or intimidate, they had come for his head, and they were actually trying to unhinge the gate.

He saw what looked like a lorry they had come in and more were alighting from the rear; he called for his guards to rally to the house and one of them let the dogs out; probably the gardener. The gates came off slightly letting in a handful of the attackers; they were brought down by the guards which only infuriated the others more. Suddenly without warning the gates crashed down and they rushed in.

Young, hefty and clearly bloodthirsty men; their eyes bloodshot, they had taken the local narcotics administered by the native doctor they were in alliance with. They were stoned to kill. The dogs didn't stand much of a chance against that crowd; the guards fought fiercely then the battle was concentrated on the balcony stairway; it was like a small riot on the front porch – more than twenty men having a go at only three men.

Chief Kobimdi fought like a wounded beast, some supernatural force must have given him the strength of many as he stabbed; slashed; shot; and dodged till he exhausted his bullets, and his guards were equally formidable. Only one was left and the attackers a lot fewer than they were when they came. Blood, body parts, smashed in eye sockets - the carnage was uncalled for, yet there was no sense of remorse on either side; whatever caught what; cut what.

One would wonder, where their neighbors were and where the police was.

The guard forced him to his back and told him to run for his life and save his family, at this point they were his best friends. Yet even they were impressed, to them he was a true warrior. The assailants climbed up behind them onto the stairway so that Desmond's father and his guard were trapped between them. He was ready for them, he felt water running down all over his body and knew it was blood, mostly his, it didn't stop him nonetheless. They cut, stabbed and hit at him, his family was in danger and to get to them they would have to pass through him, he finished off those guys and turned round to find all his guards were down. He was all alone, where were his neighbors, the police, to hell with them this was his war and the last thing he would do was to run from it or have others fight it for him; he might have done a couple of things wrong but these had no right to dispose of his son and expected child, so he faced them with all the strength he had left in him; he knew this was the end, he screamed like his ancestor who cut off his leg to scare away invaders must have done. The scream must have been rather impressive and equally stunning because the attackers seemed to fall back in surprise so that he drove right into them and flesh started flying around; his flesh their flesh, something hit him like a punch and there was a flash before his eyes; he turned round to face the source and with all the energy he had he ripped the man in two. Suddenly he realized he was falling but not knowing why until he hit the stairs. The funny thing was they didn't touch him until he reached the ground and they rushed upstairs into the house stepping on him, the hill had been take; Desmond's father tried not to close his eyes even as they stepped all over him, he overheard them shouting.

"Odogwu ka i bu, this man is a warrior!"

"Is it only this man we've been struggling to pass through since?"

Chief Kobimdi smiled.

They went into his house and found nothing because they came out hissing and cursing out of frustration and gave a few more kicks to his body.

One of them shouted. "His family is gone, the bastard …!"

Chief smiled again and released himself to the darkness that was engulfing him.

At the Ladipo Bateye junction of the G.R.A, Desmond and his mother were still trying to stop cars for help; but the trouble with the G.R.A at that time of the night is the very light traffic, people get very scared when seemingly strange people who look like beggars are trying to flag them down, as senior civil servants they also tend to mind their business absolutely at least till the trouble is over (of course double locking their gates). Hence help wasn't their next-door neighbor, nor the next car passing. They heard voices behind them.

Desmond urged his mother faster, he saw the lights of an approaching vehicle, out of desperation he jumped into its front forcing it to screech to a halt. It was a painted taxi cab. Pointing the gun at the driver, he urged his mother to board it. Still at gun point which might not have been really necessary he held the driver until his mother entered, by now some of the mob had come into view Desmond fired some shots at them then issued instructions to the driver and shouted,

"GO NOW! Will meet you there somehow."

As the Taxi sped off the mob rushed at him again and he fired once more in their direction; one of them screamed, at that opportunity Desmond ran into the bush nearby. He had the advantage of familiarity with the GRA neighborhood, which his pursuers didn't have.

As soon as he made it through several compounds, he was at the rail crossing, he ran and darted across the road until he saw a 'Molue' bus and forced himself in with the teeming crowd.

He kept jumping off and onto buses that night not sure if he was still being chased or if he was just seeing shadows. He felt the best thing was to lead them as far away from his mother as he could. He had no idea the chase stopped after he crossed the railway line. That night, on getting to 'Mile 2', he boarded a bus illegally and then fell asleep oblivious to the fact that it was going to Cotonou in Benin Republic!

Not long after Desmond and his assailants left their street a dark blue Volkswagen beetle car drove by and stopped where the Fiat lorry had been opposite the gate, the place was deserted apart from bodies lying all over the place and the smoldering ruins of the gate-house. The main house was still reasonably intact apart from the broken doors and smashed windows and the burning stairway.

The driver of the beetle car was a Caucasian male and quite huge, actually an Irish Catholic Priest; Desmond's former Principal. He was shocked and made the sign of the cross as he stepped over mutilated bodies with his big shoes. He had served as a Chaplain in the US Army, he had his own fair share of mutilated bodies, but this was unexpected yet he proceeded into the compound searching for a sign of life and preferably a familiar face.

He had forgotten the reason why he had driven all the way from Kano and the letter in his car. He still couldn't understand what led to such carnage. He stopped for a moment and wondered if he had entered the wrong compound.

The letter was an award to Desmond, a full scholarship to study engineering at the Massachusetts Institute for Technology. He saw a familiar looking corpse and bent down over it, it was Desmond's father the Priest felt for his pulse which was very weak, he went round inspecting other bodies looking for Desmond and his mother, fruitless he ran back and picked up Desmond's father cursing in the process and headed for his car which was easy for him being that he was a big man. As he drove away, he could hear sirens whining in the distance behind him.

Desmond was lost. He didn't understand why or how. One moment he was being chased by people who could have easily been his uncles or playmates when he visited the village. All because of a girl he barely even knew, they had never even been alone together; he had never even entertained any thoughts of affection towards her, heck he wouldn't have even picked her as one of his top 10 closest female friends. Yet he had brought all this outrage and disaster upon his family.

He had not the faintest inkling that it was the bride who had suggested him as the proxy groom; he would never know that she had nursed a crush for him and had silently wished, as a matter of fact wanted to be his girlfriend and now she saw an opportunity to be his wife. Unfortunately, he had gotten married to her without knowing it.

Desmond was beaten and then arrested, no one could understand him and the little French he remembered from school days made matters worse. He had no valid travel papers; he didn't even understand where he was until he got to the police station. Fortunately, the desk sergeant could speak a little English and took pity on him. However, it appeared that a good number of young Africans were stowing away and heading towards Liberia as a route to Europe and America as refugees and wartime displaced persons. Even though he tried to explain that he was not trying to do that, the sergeant and his cell mates had made him to understand that if he tried to return to Nigeria, he would get arrested, locked up for ever or shot and dumped somewhere. He was an illegal alien and his military government had zero tolerance for such.

He spent three months working in Cotonou then headed for Liberia, he didn't know what was leading him he just boarded the first route he heard like one under some hypnotic pull towards a certain destination, except he did not know where.

He was just running away from the terror and guilt that he was responsible for killing everyone he loved; he hoped that, once he was out of the picture, they would let the rest of his family off the hook. In Liberia he stayed as another three months to work up enough money for a seat on a boat to the United States. By now very lean and dark brown; he was carrying a large loaf of bread and a plastic flask of pineapple juice which wouldn't even last him a few days but he didn't know that, his so called benefactors were not interested in his welfare or if he gets to his destination dead or alive all they wanted was his money and to fill the boat with as many illegals as possible; more buttocks, more money; life goes on.

It was their third night on the high seas, not knowing how far away from shore they were or how near to their destination or worse still that the boat was not bound for the American continent but for a slave merchant's yacht.

Just before midnight a coastal patrol team bore down on them, whether it was a mistake or premeditated they opened fire on the boat. Desmond's world was shattered as his body was thrown into the water; icy cold, salty water.

He could swim, but this was different. He felt some pressure on his head and some irritation at different parts of his body. Just irritations he thought to himself, maybe just mosquito bites. His mind started to argue with itself as to how mosquito bites was possible in the middle of the Atlantic or pacific or Mediterranean ocean. There wasn't enough time for that as the darkness swallowed him and it all went quiet.

There were no survivors found to tell of the narrow choice they had between the devil and the deep blue sea; for example, all the people in that boat would have opted for the deep blue if they'd known their actual destination.

CHAPTER 1

APRIL 1998 WEEK ONE

The country was at its knees before her military dictator. Anyone identified as an

opposition or as a voice of dissent was 'terminated decisively' in the words of the ruler; the

General. He kept that rank title as against his actual self-promoted rank of Field Marshal simply

because, he declared,

"General sounds better and more important, a Field Marshal on the other hand sounds

like an old war-beaten soldier who was too scared of the battlefield and only good for ceremonial

propaganda. It is impressive but not important unless you are the Field Marshal Head of State,

and I am both and the highest General in the continent!".

As part of the official protocol, he was formally addressed as 'The Head of State and

Chairman of the Armed Forces Ruling Council (AFRC) which he later changed to the

Provisional Ruling Council of the Armed Forces of Nigeria (PRC) in an attempt to convince that

he wanted a transition to civil democratic rule.

There had been a number of attempted and botched coup d'état against him, some were

nipped at the planning stage, others had been capped as soon as it started. Half the country

loathed him; the other half feared him. The army was mostly under his control and for every failed coup, he got better control as it was an opportunity to erase his enemies and recruit his cronies and allies.

A recently foiled coup against him led to half the cream of the nation's top brass from two regions eliminated by implication. Everyone knew it was a set-up but no one dared to speak up against it, moreover it was a military problem, they were all being destroyed by what they built.

The mockery of a transition to civil rule program which his government was supervising was like an infected sore getting infected again. The ten political parties had resolved to adopt him as their sole candidate; the whole world watched in awe while the masses groaned in pain.

The people had gotten so scared of him that they were beginning to spurn myths about him having supernatural powers to see and hear anything, anywhere, anytime. In fact, some were too scared of calling his name, lest he appeared and killed them, instead they called him General Death.

Pro-democracy activists were hunted down and arrested, some were accused of treasonable offences and executed on the spot, others were sentenced to indefinite terms at the maximum-security prisons with daily visits to the torture chambers while the lucky ones were just brutalized on arrest and locked up. Some did escape before arrest and to exile in other countries or just remained hidden in the country, living in the shadows. Poverty was at an all-time high. Only the general and his friends were the comfortable ones along with their sycophants whom he barely tolerated, the rest of the populace were nobodies 'dying' and in constant fear of their Head of States and his whims and caprices.

The general; charcoal dark skin, short and rotund sat in his private lounge wearing a scarlet caftan, it was the popular fashion of the day. The Senegalese had redesigned the jellabiya using brocade fabric and made even more popular by their top musician. It was a contemporary African style. The atmosphere in the lounge was meant to subdue anyone he entertained there, the lighting was dim, the cushions and chairs had maroon red shade, apart form that the décor was exquisite, the best in Africa. What the rest of the world, apart from his security detail and his oldest wife didn't know was that the room had been designed and retrofitted by a Czech interior decorator popular with the dictators. The air vents had unnoticeable pipes that released small doses of burning khat. It was specially prepared with wild roses so that it scented like incense whereas the occupants were inhaling psychotropic drugs. He was constantly in pain so he needed the euphoric effect, but when he received guests there, it was to make them feel whatever he wanted them to feel. His oldest wife never visited him there.

The presidential palace's interior decorations even surpassed that of the Saudi monarchy's most exquisite room, this could have been the throne room but that was somewhere else. In this room he wore no shades, the light couldn't hurt his eyes here; very few people, six actually knew of his ailment; a rare liver disease which was affecting his sight and sometimes his mind, making it necessary for him to consume opium regularly, his personal physician had told him there was hope, a slim one; they would have to get him another liver that would fit him exactly otherwise he would die either slowly from the ailment or even quicker from a a mismatch, which cost the doctor his head. They patronized witch doctors too, he even got placed on a diet to eat raw human liver harvested from a living healthy young man. Ever since, the general and his chief security adviser, Colonel Jia had been searching for a liver; some of the so-called ritual killings reported across the country were actually his men at work looking for a match. Sometimes they would lure young girls, often girls between sixteen years and twenty years old deceived with the promise of an "out of this world" party with the rich and powerful for his carnal orgies. When the girls discover who was hosting them, they get awe struck, until the ones chosen for the night's special realize they are the meal. Ten women would walk in, only six or eight might leave all roofied.

Yet nothing substantial came out of it all, even his witch doctors had nothing to offer him except more human sacrifices on the false hope to get immortality; many fed the rock with their blood.

That was months ago; he had become a cannibal, though he felt some respite for a month or two, then his condition got worse.

His wife, eldest son, that he did not kill, his chief security aide, personal physician and personal attendant all knew of his illness but so did some of the world's most powerful spy agencies too. There was another very powerful, and little-known force, the Custodians, they had placed a contract on the general.

Professor Richard Balogun sat opposite the general,

"So how much do you think you'll need for the next stage of the campaign?"

The Professor replied, "Your Excellency sir, the campaign will be in three stages, the second is to set up the association for Nigerian democracy; the third will be my stepping down and declaring support for your mandate thirty days to the elections, and organization of rallies. For now, let me have only twenty-five million Naira for the first two stages."

"OK, Prof., Jia will arrange for one of the bullion vans to escort you home with the money, are you sure it is enough?"

Professor Balogun answered, "Yes sir! Yes your Excellency sir!"

Professor Balogun was at least fifteen years older than the general; he was supposed to be the only one who stood up for his mandate and opposed the general's self-succession bid.

The professor went down on his knees in a show of gratitude, the general smiled then spoke with feigned embarrassment; waving him to get off the floor, the general asked,

"How is madam's health?"

"Ah! Your Excellency sir, if not for your quick intervention I would have been a widower",

"Haba Prof, Prof, get up and sit down,"

"I swear your Excellency sir, even god couldn't have done better!"

"That's alright, I think the first lady has something for your wife and kids. As for the Libyan delegation; ehen, your son has been made the new attaché to the Lagos Garrison General officer in Command, he is a good boy, colonel Balogun, Goodnight!"

Which was simply a dismissal command than a courtesy, the professor was still prostrating and mumbling 'thank yous' but the general had tunedoff as if there was no one there.

There was a time when he only received visitors and addressed state matters in his office, that was just a few months ago but felt like two years away. To stay up for an hour would require two days of transfusions, sacrifices and then the making up to cover the spreading patches. At some point he thought it was leprosy, thankfully it wasn't. then again, occasionally his mind would wander if the liver disease was not worse than leprosy. A part of him knew there was no cure but he entertained a dim ray of hope that a solution would be found. He couldn't get help overseas because he knew the moment, he was taken out for such, he would either be killed, abducted or exiled. There was too much at stake for him to just let things go easy. When he took power, it was a very simple objective; take over and stop the rot. Now all he did was kill enemies, amass wealth and try to stay alive so he can establish a new dictatorial monarchy of his family. He knew this country very well and no measure of progress could be made without the exercise of force by a single responsible leader who would do great good; the people had become lazy and corrupt – thanks to his predecessors.

He was right in the need to make things better and rid the nation of corruption; he was right that a strong leadership was needed to enforce the necessary change but, he was wrong; he had no good intentions and he was not a responsible leader.

Desmond parked his Volvo S40 salon car in the nearest vacant space he saw, locked, switched on the anti-burglary alarm and listened for the customary beep.

He had visited the Ikoyi club a few times with his father back in the days and quite a lot had changed ever since; the place looked well put together.

He strode to the bar wearing a white T-shirt with 'DISBANDED' inscribed on its front tucked into a pair of dark blue jeans with brushed out bottoms on a pair of black suede palm slippers. He got glances from several women as they passed him, which made him feel really good. At the bar he ordered for a glass of 'Old Fashioned' and just caught the look of approval of the barman before he turned to make the drink; it always worked anywhere.

"Boss you have very rare and excellent taste, I just hope you enjoy mine like the others you are used to abroad, around here I really don't get to do this so often."
Desmond replied, "Yes, I'd been wondering if you could deliver after I'd asked…. Wait, don't tell me, you are Ghanaian?"

The bartender smiled and nodded with a twinkle in his eye and his chest puffed with pride.

"Thank you".

Desmond collected his drink but as he was about to start drinking a hand suddenly was clasped over his eyes and he heard a voice,

"Ananse, please make as many more of that brew, he's not leaving here until daybreak. Now Doctor Desmond guess who shut out the light and you can have my girlfriend if you get it right."

Desmond couldn't guess right, eventually he was let go to face one of his old friends from his secondary school days, Michael. They both jumped at each other shouting, patting each back, shaking hands repeatedly and spinning round. When the excitement had died down, Desmond just stared at Michael; he was wearing a plain T-shirt on khaki brown shorts with a pair of athletic sandals, and a clean-shaven face. He was showing off his muscles,

"Michael you haven't changed much except that you have some extra beef now. Haba! What are you eating?"

"Looku you! You, who is looking more well fed, me or you who've been eating burgers and potatoes and ice cream, while I've been on army rations, you haven't changed much yourself"

Desmond replied, "Some army ration that must be, we aren't old yet anyway, we are still young, just big boys now, hey where are the others?"

Michael hadn't changed much, now a lieutenant colonel Micheal Oriyole of the Nigerian Army, he had been Desmond's best friend in secondary school, also had been his wingman as pack leader of their boys' club; the 'Wolfies', the toast of the school. Michael had never liked his name being shortened so he always insisted on the complete form; Michael, never Mike.

They had been eleven core members, best friends always seen together; they were the 'Form zero' generation of Nigeria. The silenced generation. A very cruel and vindictive state policy that marked the beginning of the end of academic growth in the country. An education minister under one of the past dictators dismantled the academic system and curriculum, caused the mass lay-off of university lecturers, in his words 'A lot of university teachers were teaching what they were not paid to teach.' Many teachers lost their jobs on account of that statement, and today the effects are still there. Desmond's generation would have started a new school, year and class at the end of summer in 'Form one'; then the first year of secondary school, but the change from 6-5-4 to 6-3-3-4 years at each school point created a dilemma and confusion because they had final year students with nowhere to go and new intakes with no room to come in; hence some smart schools instead of keeping their prospective students at home longer, introduced them into 'Form Zero' classes. The cascade effect continued across the system even decades after.

Out of the eleven friends; one died in their second year from a sickle cell anemia illness; another two left their school at the same stage; one turned against them leaving seven of them left till graduation. Desmond was the originator and their leader until he disappeared after his father got killed.

Of the other six; three got into the national defense academy, each passing out as- Michael in the army; Emeka Ubomi an air force combat pilot; Francis Otoluwa a naval officer; the other three one a police officer; one a lawyer and the sixth a journalist. Only Desmond ended up as a civilian engineer.

For the first time in years, they were physically together again. A brilliant Saturday afternoon reunion. Their secondary school days had been fun despite a few setbacks and the usual boy-girl disappointments. All super-hero and science project enthusiast, mixing up comic book characters with reality and chemical accidents, etc. Some called them the musketeers because they always stood up for each other; they'd been class and school prefects each distinguishing themselves for good leadership qualities.

Desmond outshone them all in these qualities. His moral objections had earned him the nickname of 'reverend father Desmond', which of course irritated him. The first time they met like this was in school, the day the 'Wolfies' was born. At this reunion, none of them remembered it had been this same day twenty years ago they formed the Wolfies club.

"Gentlemen I present to you Dr. Desmond, sorry Dr. Diamond commander in chief of the wolfies…"

Michael's intro was followed by the laughter and cheer from the other four guys sitting around. they quickly grabbed a vacant table and joined it to theirs, pushed both of them to the wall making a longer table and pulled their chairs together around it. They were a noisy bunch causing other patrons, especially the more elderly club users to give them disapproving glances, but no one dared challenge them they were military boys; they ordered for more drinks. Over the years the elitist hangouts had become extended officers' Mess especially for those with appointments in the corridors of power. The regulars were kept within the confines of standard Mess.

"OK guys, emmmm, we have here Lawrence Ayinde aka Lance, press secretary to the Lagos state military administrator; Barrister Gerald Enda an attorney with the Ovie and Robson law firm; Superintendent of Police (SP or SuPol) John Joseph also called Jojo by most officers and close friends; Squadron Leader Emeka Ubomi of the Nigerian Airforce; hey, where is Frank…?"

Michael was interrupted as they all turned to face Frank standing there, mouth agape;

"It's a lie, no way! Hey I know you, you mother …, sorry, father Desmond, Yellow, diamond"

He stamped to close his heels pushing out his chest in a mock 'civvies' salutation, which by the way didn't click as he was wearing sneakers, and stood at attention for Desmond. This was an extraordinary show of respect and affection as the military never salutes a civilian. Even though it was a comic gesture it would only be done within such a close-knit company of friends with an overwhelming number of military officers. To onlookers they were all soldier boys. Even

Desmond still had the air of a serving military man. Desmond stood up and was lifted off his feet by the taller and bigger Frank.

Clearing his throat, Michael continued his introduction

"Ahem! This is lieutenant commander Francis Otoluwa of NNS Bayajidda of the most prestigious navy in Africa"

As they sat down and greetings circulated Desmond cleared his throat and spoke,

"And I am Desmond Kobimdi ex US-marine Captain, engineering corps, at your service gentlemen."

And they all guffawed.

After a while Desmond noticed they had become a nuisance and suggested they go somewhere else and Frank spoke, "Why don't we have a small party, a reunion party?"

Lance asked where and somebody suggested the beach, Alpha beach which met the consent of the others, Gerald said

"We can get some food and snacks from any of the restaurants around or we could leave that for the ladies to sort out,"

That suggestion equally met with their consent. Frank then asked, "So na who go bring fresh fish?" Referring in slang to the lady escorts. Desmond looked lost and Frank offered to decode,

"Where we can get the best girls in…,"

Desmond didn't let him finish, shaking his head violently, "Ooooh, No! Guys I don't do prostitutes!"

"Ah, sorry o, 'Fada" Desmond, no I didn't mean that, actually my girlfriend is studying at the university of Lagos, we could organize something with her friends." Was Emeka's response.

Fada was a colloquial way of referring to a Reverend Father, they used it to tease Desmond as a young teenager because of his strict conservative Christian upbringing.

Desmond thought so too; it was the same even in more conservative Nigeria, wherever you see men in uniform there'll always be undergrads not too far off. He also thought it was true all he had learned about the university campuses, especially the ivy-leagues, he asked

"This place, is it Moremi hall?"

"Wow, so you already know about l'hotel d'morems." Chipped in Gerald.

"Yes, my cousin, is a student there in his final year, engineering", replied Desmond.

Outside in the parking lot they split into three groups; Michael and Desmond in his Volvo while the other five went in the two Prado jeeps which caught Desmond's attention as they headed for the university. While on the way Desmond inquired from Michael how Frank and Emeka could afford the cars and he let Desmond know that all officers above the rank of Major each had one. They had come as good will gifts form the head of state to key and elite military officers especially the young and more dangerous ones, this he did frequently to keep their teeth stuck in his pie so that they would remain loyal to him; and no one dared reject them or die foolishly and get implicated in some treasonable offence or be sent to Bakassi peninsula to fight Cameroonian insurgents. Michael gave him a quick rundown on the state of the nation which was a pathetic story; all those dreams and fantasies they'd nursed as school children about a great nation with young heroes like them pushing the frontiers suddenly felt very childish and naive.

Getting to the university campus for the second or third time in his life Desmond wondered where all the students had gone to, as if reading his thoughts Michael told him that on weekends like this most of the students would have gone home or holed up in their rooms attending to either assignments or doing long put off domestic chores.

He vaguely remembered the very rare visits to see his uncle, a professor and some of his cousins. Once you drove through those gates, you were transformed into another world. It was like a border crossing into a first-world country; a highly cosmopolitan environment, with European type suburban houses and pockets of students walking, studying, discussing like any ivy-league university in England or America. It was a community one aspired, dreamed of joining, so you worked very hard to get there and become one of the super-mortals. Traveling overseas to study was not the preferred option, except someone offered to pay you for it. Now looking around, it all seemed like a lifetime ago. The structures, landscape and students he was seeing didn't look so intriguing.

Desmond made his first stop at his cousin's dormitory and gave him some money to take his friends out on a treat. Konwe was beside himself with excitement; it was always a good thing to be visited by a Yankee (US based) or Jand (UK based) friend or relative, it gave a student bragging rights and an extraordinary swag to be differentiated from regular mortals. Unfortunately, it also meant being under the radar of the university ganglands and secret cult groups, unless you've become an untouchable. You can either be needed for funding, political connections or as a poster-boy to attract other recruits or girls. An untouchable was either a 'toxic' student or a student connected at a very high level that is either anti-cult or much stronger cult.

At Moremi hall the cars were carefully and strategically parked in a way such that they had a fenced off triangle giving them a spacious enclosure and some semblance of privacy so that they could continue with other conversation while Emeka and Michael went up to get the girls. Desmond looked at his wrist watch and was surprised that it had gotten so late into the day but he as soon shrugged it off and looked forward to what the only Nigerian University of his choice over fifteen years ago could offer him now. Deep down he was afraid he would be disappointed or even pleased which could only mean a threat to his sense of morality, the girl would probably want to sleep with him which meant she was public property and that he wasn't going to be a party to, how did he ever, survive abroad with this old-fashion way of looking at sex, he was as straight as they came from his generation. He was good with the ladies, he could almost certainly get a date when he asked, yet he was very particular about who he asked and for what. His past life sometimes made him walk a very thin line; crossed that thin line and he'd suffered the consequences quietly and painfully. Most people saw him as a stud, a player. And that he was.

F-block was for the very private occupants of Moremi Hall, not as boisterous and public as the other wings. It housed the student executives too. If you weren't meant to be there, you'd stand out like a sore thumb and even though privacy was the premium, everyone knew who belonged there and who didn't. It was the reserved area and both the rich and not so poor were accommodated there, everyone knew to mind their business conveniently unless of course your room mates were your type. If you didn't want people in your business or your business in people, F-block was the place to be, if you applied early enough or found a more extroverted person willing to swap or sell their space.

F206 was an OK room except that it was divided into four bed space cubicles so that each of the occupants could have their own stereo, TV refrigerator, reading desk spaces apart from their bed space.

Each cubicle had a second occupant known as a squatter so that the total population of the room was eight. A squatter could be a rent paying second or third occupant or just a fortunate free-loader. There were times when they would really step on each other's fingers more like but they were really good friends when certain things like cleaning up, religion or morality weren't being discussed. There were two nominal Moslems, a new age Christian, two Anglicans and the rest Catholics. one Moslem and one Catholic came from quite humble civil service parents; Sophia was in her final year law and a 4.49 GPA which meant law school would come with a lot more pressure for her to confirm her mettle; Amina was a second-year student of Biochemstry; Sophia's best friend was Ronke; daughter of one of the old money bag families of Lagos now in hibernation during the dictatorship. Ronke was Emeka's girlfriend, a Catholic but a spoilt brat. It was only under a military rule that an igbo and a Yoruba from such a distinguished family could have such a relationship without serious consequences. Her parents had tried but two things worked in their favour; Emeka was a senior army officer and Ronke was her dad's only daughter, he did whatever he could to make her happy. If having this soldier as her toy-boy would keep her happy then so be it. Also, it was not a bad thing to have a few army boys watching over them and helping out from time to time. He hoped, though she would out-grow him like she did with most obsessions.

The other two girls were Business Administration finalists, the sixth girl was Michael 's girl, an extra year for maternity reasons which Michael owned up to; the other Moslem an Electrical Engineering third year student and the last girl a Psychology finalist. This particular Saturday the gang was complete and they were chattering away as they shared a two hundred and fifty-Naira suya.

Sophia found it hard to concentrate on her term paper which had to do with the Geneva Conventions of 1949 and their Additional Protocols. She didn't realize until that moment that there are four conventions and sixty-four articles. People always threw the phrase around and made it sound like some paragraph or bullet points like the 'Ten Commandments' but, it was actually volumes and volumes to digest. She didn't know where to start from and besides she could only find the second and the fourth conventions in the library. Stuffing some more suya into her mouth she plugged her ears with Walkman earphones and faced her reading desk while the music was playing. In front of her there were six thick additional volumes of reviews and critics and cases on the subject from the library and the paper was due the following Wednesday. Her friends teased her and Ronke shouted,."Don't worry I'll look for trouble that will mature by the time you are called to the bar!"

They all laughed. They were talking about clothes, then shifted to skin care and hairstyles eventually they ended up talking about men when Emeka and Michael knocked on their door. As they came in the two girls jumped on their boyfriends while the others were glad because this meant some distraction to counter boredom, grub and extra pocket money. It was a known fact that most of the well-connected military officers carried stacks of cash and weapons in their vehicle trunks. It was also amazing how very few cases of them being robbed were ever known.

Emeka quickly told them of their plans for the weekend, Ronke sent them out of the room so she could have a quick girl's meeting and hopefully convince the pack to join in.

She asked them to wait down stairs and started to convince the other girls to join in the fun which would have been a smooth task if not for Sophia's refusal on the pretext that she had too much work on her hands. After much coercing and bluffing on the part of Ronke, Sophia accepted more out of a sense of responsibility to watch over Ronke but with a condition that she would back out if she didn't like the looks of the other guys and if she did go with them, they would be back by seven at night. Besides her boyfriend had gone home for the weekend to visit his parents so there'd be less of an awkward situation if he came to see her and she had gone out with her friends, especially since she had requested not to be disturbed because she had a load of coursework.

Sophia tried to be courteous to everyone, somehow, she had been fixed up with Desmond or they naturally gravitated towards each other.

'The two 'oyinbos', Ronke had referred to them as. Of the lighter skinned ladies, she was the lightest in complexion just shy of albinism and so was Desmond. In fact, her initial thought was a half-caste man or a Mid-Eastern man, her curiosity had led to attraction. Being caught in the act made her upset and she tried to hide behind a veiled hostility but subtle enough to not be disruptive.

Sophia sat beside him as they drove out of the University headed to the beach. Desmond noticed her masked hostility and didn't need to be told that she didn't approve of the gathering or of him, suddenly he became angry too and slammed on the breaks meaning to take her back to her hostel but thought better of it recalling what Ronke had told him;

"Please treat my friend well she is like a nun… and she takes life too seriously, she needed a break from all the books she's been reading. I trust you'll be a gentleman, she's not bush meat o!".

Everyone queried him for the sudden stop while other road users poured invectives at him, he apologized and continued driving; Sophia said to him

"If you do that more often you would spend all your money on fixing cars in Lagos."

Desmond looked at her and smiled then said,

"I'm sorry err.."

She helped him;

"…Sophia, that's my name."

Desmond relaxed a bit. "Sophia, I don't really know my way around could you point me in the right direction to Alpha beach? These my friends have forgotten I'm new to driving in this city and I can't keep up with their speed just now."

She looked at him and smiled then said an "OK".

At the beach they had a marvelous time that even Sophia forgot all her hesitations. At a point the ladies were doing their own thing while the men were on their own and got into talk about the country again, then Gerald said as an alcohol assisted joke;

"For a change may be what we do need in this country is a civilian coup."

And they all started laughing. Suddenly Desmond's countenance changed and he said,

"Yes, guys maybe we should have another coup but a civilian one!"

This was followed by silence since no one really knew what to say; it was Lance who broke the silence when he said,

"Yeah maybe you Desmond should start it; I propose a toast to the first civilian coup ever!"

They all raised their beer bottles, clinked them together and started laughing again. It was a good joke under the circumstances but they each had a strange feeling that they had just started something for real.

The sun was going down and they gathered their things and headed for Desmond's hotel. On the way Sophia fell asleep in the car. At the hotel she woke up, it wasn't until she had gotten over the initial awe of Desmond' s hotel suite that she saw the time on the wall clock and screamed,

"Oh my God look at the time! It's half past nine, Ronke!"

Her friend was already dancing with the others ignoring her. Sophia walked straight to her and pulled her aside. Desmond looked at his watch then looked up to see Sophia and Ronke were having an argument. Ronke didn't let her embarrassment show rather she dragged Sophia to where Desmond was standing.

"Here, oga! She's your date, take care of her and please keep her to yourself!"

Before Sophia could utter another word, Desmond quickly offered to take her back to the university which took her unawares and disarmed her completely, her stiffened back and raised shoulders suddenly gave way and she sighed then headed for the door.

On the drive back to her Unilag campus, Desmond apologized to Sophia for any inconveniences they might have caused her and she opened up to him about her academic work load; the term paper; the recent abductions and ritual killings and her family; what her father would do to her if he should hear about her exploits. She skipped the part about her boyfriend.

Such fears he admitted he hadn't heard of for a while. Eventually he offered to help her with the term paper. She looked at him puzzled.

"How can you, an engineer help me with a final year law coursework? What would you know about such?"

He quickly explained how he had worked with the military and it was a mandatory pre-deployment requirement to take the courses on GCAP and ROEs. She was lost and asked'

"What's GCAP and ROE?"

"It stands for Geneva Conventions and additional Protocols and other Rules of Engagement".

He didn't tell her though, that he was more than an engineering contractor. What had nearly become a wild misadventure turned out to be a heaven sent. They drove to the Law

Faculty after she had gathered all required study materials from her room. They couldn't have worked in her room since all male visitors were refused entry after ten at night, moreover Desmond was not ready to enter the place. They worked all night till early morning then had a short break talking about each other over a flask of sweetened black coffee until Sophia looked at his watch and found it had stopped, he took it off and was about to start fixing it when Sophia started groaning about her tooth, this got worse that in his haste Desmond dropped his watch in her bag and ran out to his car where he retrieved a tooth ache reliever gel, which was in a first aid kit he always kept in his cars. On his return he made her open her mouth while he administered a few squirts of the golden yellow pineapple flavored gel. Without saying anything else Desmond helped her back to her dormitory, still politely avoiding to get inside, Sophia sensed he was afraid because of the way he stared at the place as they approached the main gates, he tried to hide it but he looked scared of the place; that was quite strange and adorable at the same time. She didn't know when she chuckled and, in an attempt, to hide it, placed her head on his shoulder then quickly pulled back again.

When he got back to his hotel all his friends were asleep, it was half past ten Sunday morning, stepping over them he headed for his room, while undressing he remembered his wrist watch but couldn't figure out where he'd left it he swore under his breathe, crossed over to the bathroom and after a warm bath to remove the salt from his body, he went to bed, he had to be in Church for Mass in the evening.

Konwe had been looking for an opportunity to ask Osa out for the past two years. He'd known her, she was his friend; actually, she had been his junior in the Chaplaincy's International Red Cross Society. For the first year he had totally ignored her like she was his responsibility and he was a big brother always looking out for her and favoring her as such. That was easy,

then she got into her second year in Biochemistry, became older and he started to notice her.

She'd always treated him with respect and awe, many did. But she was different, there

was an occasion when they had gone to work at an accident scene near the university and it was

raining; she was drenched and cold so he had to take off his shirt for her to wear, at the end of

the whole exercise the shirt had been blood stained, when they got back to the campus she

insisted on washing it herself before returning it to him. She did just that. He could inspire her to

do things that not even the elder sister could make her do. When he realized he was attracted to

her and wanted a more serious relationship with her he became insecure. He didn't know what to

do about it and there was no one to ask for advice, not even his father. It was not usual for boys

to ask their father's or mother's for advice on women – you were a guy; you figure it out

yourself. On the contrary, most women did get mentored and coached from as early in their

girlhood even onto advanced womanhood.

Given time, Konwe got over the personal struggle over his feelings. Was it right to feel

this way about a girl? Was he taking advantage of her trust feeling this way? And all the other

floods of conflict in his young head? Now he longed for an opportunity to ask her out. To him,

the opportunities he sought, were more like excuses. His friends didn't help much either, they

were aware of his feelings as he chose not to hide it from them. Sometimes they would tease him

as being hooked on a 'senior jambite' as a reference to one who had just been promoted out of

her sophomore year, when he could spread his tentacles and catch as many babes as his net could

hold. Konwe and his friends who were mostly his roommates were sex shy but liked girls as

much as any other young normal boys of their age and that was a difficult balance to maintain in a culture of moral rebellion and sexual adventure as was their generation's but survive it they did, at a price of course.

The black sheep of the group who had lost out in the fight was their fourth friend, Nduka; being a player by choice; since a player without balls for game would be like an action movie without violence, he had to opt for live action. A saying goes, that two things can put a man into trouble; money and women. Konwe used half the money his uncle gave to him to take his friends out to one of the university campus restaurants; Osa was with them too. They all had a wonderful time and soon headed back to their hostels. His friends had their own visits to make too so they all walked Osa back to her hostel. Sensing that Konwe and Osa needed some time alone the other three excused themselves and continued on their 'ward rounds'.

At first it was difficult for Konwe to express himself maybe because he hadn't rehearsed his lines properly, but as soon as his heart beat rate reduced, he let loose like a master orator; at the end of it Osa told him she wasn't ready for such a relationship, afraid that her heart would get broken. Konwe approached it from different angles short of begging her, it was getting pathetic. One thing that touched Osa was the way he made a joke of it all so that people who saw them from a distance or caught drifts of their conversation would conclude they were two lovers and the boy was asking forgiveness for some offence committed.

In the very near future, Osa would revisit that evening in her mind very often for hours un-end before she died. What her life may have been like if she had said yes to him. The truth wasn't really her fear of a heart break; she couldn't bring herself to tell Konwe that though she liked him, he was what they called a 'nice guy'. She was already hanging out with a 'bad guy'. Konwe was her anecdote or band aid whenever she needed one. Probably if she had said yes to him that night, she would have been on the right side of campus the night that landed her in the

ER. She would have been with Konwe or someplace else boring but safe; she wouldn't have ended up drugged, raped and dead as a doornail some months later because of the 'bad-guy' who promised her a thrill ride, and if she did say yes Konwe might not have been prepared for the pain her disguised and fraudulent escapades with the 'big boys' that his 'loving senses' couldn't have perceived. It was common place for young girls and ladies to pass-up dating young men who genuinely liked them for the thrill of being with much older men or gang bangers and popular kids. The attraction to danger and violence was slowly becoming a socio-cultural problem but it was an invincible problem because the girl had been made invincible by society in these parts. Sometimes a young lady would have two boyfriends; one was the academic bodyguard or 'car washer' as was often called while the real boyfriend 'car owner' or 'car driver' would show up whenever he wanted and she would easily dump the former to be with the latter; often unceremoniously and without apologies.

Eventually when they had stopped laughing together and she had rebuffed all his advances telling him not to worry that she was sure that he would find someone else, after all she knew he was quite capable.

CHAPTER 2

WEEK THREE

Retired Police Inspector Terfa had made much progress on the where abouts of Desmond's father and was very close to finding him, the only disturbing things were; one he wasn't the only one making inquiries because at the last place he checked one of the people he spoke with had asked if what he told "them" wasn't enough, two, there had been a 504 station wagon car parked near his office for some days now and he recognized it as a State Security Service (SSS) vehicle which didn't make any sense.

That morning before he left for Desmond's hotel they were gone. He had given Desmond his latest report including audio recordings of interviews he made and was about to ask for his advance when the cellular phone on Desmond's writing desk beeped. Desmond took the call; it was from Michael, there was trouble;

"Desmond, man, that bastard is at it again…"

In the rush of words, he gathered that the state administrator had been killed in a car bombing and his press secretary, Lance had been detained by the SSS in connection with the murder. When Desmond dropped the phone, he looked pale causing Terfa to inquire but he just mumbled something about the IRA; it made no sense to Terfa, he tried to question Desmond but he was stopped by the polite raising of his palm and a fake smile. He paid Terfa and dismissed him.

Terfa had spent twenty-five years of his life as a policeman from a constable. He had taken a risk and attended night school in order to get a degree only to be told it wouldn't count in the police force since he got in as a non-degree holder. In the last ten years, he had seen the military dictatorships decimate and render the Force into paralysis; they became bribe takers and checkpoint toll collectors. People would spit at them and curse at them. He barely managed to get promoted past Sergeant to Inspector, he had to bribe for his CO to write a poor commendation so that he wouldn't get stuck as a Sergeant Major. A bullet to the leg during a drug bust sealed the deal for him. To believe he had declined working that case, only for him to be assigned mysteriously to the case. There were rumors it was meant to be an ambush for him, he wasn't meant to come out of it alive. First shot got him in the leg, then just as the criminal was about to finish him off, the rifle jammed, then he fired back and that was the game changer. They made the biggest bust of drugs and cache of arms that implicated some police and military personnel. They got the firing squad; he got the promotion. After 3 years, he knew he couldn't go on and put in for a voluntary retirement. Fortune still smiled on him and they let him off with a hefty package and his pension.

Reminiscing over the events around this job and the SSS trailing him, he knew something was up with the client or his query. Well maybe because he's an American, the government was very suspicious of Americans. He would be careful. Jobs like this do not come often for people like him; it was highly needed and unexpected earnings and the additional excitement of being a detective again. This job alone would cover his two oldest children's university expenses for their remaining semesters and he would still have some extra for himself.

Later in the day Michael came around and gave him a more detailed report on the events that led to the arrest of their friend Lance;

"Word is out that the general is taking out potential threats again, I think Lance and his boss got caught up in it. Right now, he is under house arrest in one of the SSS offices in the city, he is likely to be handed over to DMI if they do not plan to take him out. If he's kept with SSS for longer, then he's fate is sealed. Yellow we have to do something!"

Desmond's reply was more of exasperation at his friend.

"We? what do you mean we? Do what precisely?! Look we can't do anything or else we too will get caught in whatever this is, we don't even know what Lance was involved in, let us wait and see…or, wait a minute, isn't Lance a civilian? Why not get him a good lawyer? Surely he can't be court martialed?!"

Michael interrupted him. "Wait?! Lawyer?! What are you talking about, we should wait and see his corpse, boy this is Nigeria under a dictator not the United States!"

"Now easy ol' boy, what do you suggest we do, go and bail him or break into the place?"

Eventually Michael listened to common sense and left the hotel not long after.

Two days later Terfa arrived at Desmond's suite with a feeling of excitement.

"Sir I have some good news and bad news, but for the bad news I'll have to start with the good; I have found your father at least from the clues I have now, the bad news is that I have lost him again or where he is now I can't get at him but I know he is there".

"You mean he is dead?"

Said Desmond; his voice beginning to crack.

"No sir. I gather your father's name is Kanayo, Osmond, Kobimdi, okay, he had changed his name to K.O. Bimdi and opened a farm a little way out of the city. I was able to locate his office at Apapa Port area, where he also has a business center for commercial photocopying, typing, international calls and computer services are carried out. No one really knows much about him except for some civil war stories he used to explain his scars. Well I guessed right when I checked it out based on the information, I already had on him. They said he had a very close friend who visited him regularly, a White Catholic Priest. However, his guest had not been sighted or visited nearly a year now; he was a former principal to a secondary school…,"

"Don't tell me," Desmond chipped in,

"I know, Saint Thomas' in Kano,"

"Yes! Now, today I was supposed to meet with him but on my way, fortunately I used public transport, I saw some security men bundling him into their vehicle…,"

Desmond cut him short. "What do you mean security men, the Priest or my father? Cops or who?"

His heart was racing and just like the first time he got caught under fire, his jugular and temple were pounding like his vessels would erupt.

"No not cops, not the police, it's the state security boys; SSS. I think your father must have messed with some military big guy, and that is the bad news."

It took a while before Desmond moved and when he did, he brought out his cheque book to pay the sergeant.

Terfa wanted his money differently, he wanted the money paid to his bank directly.

"Just to be on the safe side sir, I have this strange feeling and my instincts hardly fail me. The hotel has a cash office for guests on the ground floor, maybe you can do a telex transfer for me or pay the cheque into my account directly, this money is big and the cheque too heavy for me to carry just like that around the city."

He said this smiling and Desmond without objecting went with him to the cash office where he made the payment under the satisfied observation of Terfa. They shook hands and they each left.

On getting to the ground floor reception area of the hotel Terfa suddenly felt a chill all over his body; it was his instincts warning him again and he decided to take a different public transport route back to his flat which doubled as his home and office, and maybe catch some useful intel on the way and catch up on the day's news too. When he got the job, he felt it was best to get a small self-contained flat on the Lagos Island so he would be free from family distractions as well as protect his own identity and family. It wasn't because he suspected foul play or expected any trouble, but the turn of events and the shadow of SSS operatives crossing his path was making him increasingly glad he got an operational space away from his family. He had barely stepped away from the hotel gates when the same Peugeot car that he had been seeing pulled up in front of him as if to run him over, blocking his path at the same time making him to jump back. In the process the doors swung open, two men; one from the rear and the other from the front jumped down, grabbed him and bundled him into the back of the car. The entire operation wasn't more than five seconds.

In the rear of the car his captives had started beating and threatening him;

"You if you move a muscle, we will kill you now!"

He was shaken and terribly afraid. It was easy to imagine these things but now he was experiencing it and just didn't know what was going to happen next. Then he realized that the two men closest to him had no guns pointing at him, even if they did, it was not practical to use their submachine guns at such close range so they were banking on paralysis by fear and maybe a club or some other blunt weapon. Even if they tried to reach for their pistols, which should have been pulled from the start, they wouldn't be able to execute that move in the confined space they were all sharing. The men in the back were burly and wore trench coats which meant even less space for an armed response. How his mind overcame the terror he felt and quickly analyzed his predicament would always be a mystery to him.

Terfa remembered the paper wrap of snuff – nicotine powder he had bought for the newspaper vendor on his street; that snuff always gave him access to as many newspapers as he wanted to read and the wife would arrange for some buckets of water every day for his use.

From his side pocket, Terfa produced the paper wrapped crack and tore it open while throwing its content into the face of the nearest operative in the eyes, nose and mouth as he shielded his face with one arm while he gave the other an elbow smashing in his nose and top incisors. Terfa reached for the nearest gun and blasted the head of the guy in front who was by now reaching for him spreading his brains in the process. A struggle ensued between Terfa, the driver and the officer beside him who had by now unholstered his side-arm. The car swerved suddenly running into the side of an oil tanker that its driver was oblivious of the goings on in the car, causing it to turn over; at that instant Terfa climbed further backwards into the trunk, kicking and throwing his fist at everything and everywhere as he climbed and fell into the third row then started to slam at the rear windshield until he kicked out the rear glass of the station wagon and jumped out of the car now skidding along the road in tow with the tanker. Other cars tried to avoid the rolling body of Terfa,leading to multiple collisions. Picking himself up quickly he ran back the way he had come to the hotel as the tanker exploded behind him.

Desmond wasn't in the habit of keeping in touch with his family whenever he was on his long national assignments or his business trips in fact, he hated doing that. It took his mother and sister two years to get used to it after he brought them to the US to live with him. They never knew what he really did between when he left the Marines and before he got his lecturing appointment at the Texas University where he eventually got his doctorate degree, all they knew was he provided engineering services to industries. Now he had a consultancy firm he'd set up with some old colleagues, so they knew he wasn't a conman or into drugs.

His sister wasn't a little girl anymore and had become suspicious especially after she had come across one of his undercover international passports that identified him as a British citizen, he had to tell her that he once did some work for the CIA but eventually the project was canceled and he never went on the mission. The next day he carried out a quick cleanup of the room and made her promise not to tell anyone not even their mother. She was getting ready for university on the path to become a neuro surgeon. Tonight, he was going to call her just to reassure her that he was not getting into any trouble. He heard banging on his door, which became persistent and he had to lie to his sister that he was in a meeting with a client and had to run. So, he dropped the phone and went for the door, as he turned the handle, Terfa burst in knocking Desmond down and pinned him to the ground shouting,

"What the hell have you gotten me into Dr. Desmond, the SSS just arrested me as a coup plotter!"

What followed happened so fast that all Terfa knew was that he had lost consciousness. It was a technique a Chinese frog catcher had taught Desmond once; how they put frogs to sleep before slitting them open. By the time Terfa came to, Desmond had dressed his wounds. He listened as Terfa recounted his close shave with the state bogey men.

Desmond telephoned Michael and asked him to bring the other guys to meet him at his hotel room.

There were four new faces which made Desmond uncomfortable but after Michael reassured him, he let it go.

They were Emeka's younger brother - Azuka, he was a lieutenant with the Nigerian Army Intelligence Corps (NAIC) an offshoot from the directorate of military intelligence (DMI). The general used them to infiltrate the military while he used the SSS to terrorize the people. The DMI was also used for some highly classified military operations in and around the West African sub region. In the general's words, 'Any insurgence that lasts more than forty-eight hours under his watch has the hand government in it' Whether he meant his own hands or mutineers in his ranks, was best left to the favoured interpretation of the person facing the barrel. So, he made sure his intel was solid even if cooked by him.

Other of Michael's friends in the room included an attaché to the Lagos Garrison General officer in Command, lieutenant Colonel Benjamin Balogun; Felix Amokpai a lieutenant with the Western Armored Brigade and Sergeant Terfa who had now come under full radar of the SSS.

Desmond went ahead to explain the reason why he had called them there and asked them for suggestions on what to do.

Azuka wanted them to help Lance escape before he got killed as the instruction from the Presidential Palace was to eliminate everyone even remotely fingered with the dead governor. What that meant too was that they kept no records of collateral damage, Lance was just an inconvenience they needed to eliminate not because there was any evidence of his involvement. Lance was a civilian reporter who found favor with the governor and became his softer-friendly liaison with the press; he was never really in the main-flow of the military administration; he was just a poster boy.

How they were supposed to achieve it was the problem. As if he had rehearsed it before Desmond took over the meeting and started to give them options. At last they agreed to a jailbreak for their friend, the human rights activists would never be able to get him out, neither was legal action a way out.

He assigned duties to each person and asked them to report any useful information back to him and Michael immediately they got it.

Lt Azuka was to keep them informed on the DMI's targets as well as to find the whereabouts of Lance but not to make any contact with him.

Desmond was still trying to say something when they heard a knock on the door of his suite; very soft unmistakably female, which made everyone to stiffen and draw their sidearms. Desmond went for the door and was surprised to find Sophia standing there and she pushed something to him, his watch saying,

"Hi, I'm sorry if I was…,"

"Who is it?!"

Called out Michael from the adjoining room, with a hint of alarm in his voice.

"It is Sophia, Ronke's friend, my friend." Sophia gave him a look he didn't understand.

Desmond replied still staring at her, she murmured and made a face,

"Ronke's friend? Right"

He invited her in and tried to correct himself,

"My friend, I said my friend, he needed to understand it is you…." And he rolled his eyes as she spoke

"Sorry if I am interrupting anything, forgot found your watch in my bag, you must have dropped it at some point. I found it there this morning and… I'll be going back to the campus now," and she stopped in the middle of his sitting room,

"By the way thanks for the term paper, my lecturer actually gave me nine out of ten. Goodnight."

And she made to leave.

"No, wait please come in and stay, I will take you back to the campus, besides its already dark, these days a girl shouldn't be alone on Lagos streets at night."

She entered into room and was wondering what all of the men were doing there together and in full uniform; it wasn't her business she thought, they shouldn't get her involved in any trouble, she was just a student after all.

Without being told, they knew the meeting was adjourned and it was their cue to leave, and they all left except Michael who offered to drive Sophia and Desmond to her university in his Prado.

At the hostel car park area, some mean looking youngsters had gathered in a corner beside one of the cubicle type makeshift convenience stores. They belonged to one of the cult groups and were pulling hard on their cigarettes. Three of them accosted Desmond and started trying to extort money from him threatening that noncompliance would be terrible for him. They came sauntering and scowling with sunglasses on at night, gang insignia on their clothes and specific colors same across all three and their cohorts near the shed. They were trying very hard, in Desmond's opinion to look intimidating. He remembered one of the neighborhoods he'd lived in through his early years in America – gangland territories and he wondered why any right-thinking undergrad would want to have that as a way of life; it was a paradox really. You went to school, university to escape such a terminal affliction and be connected to life and a world of bountiful opportunities. Desmond couldn't make out what they were saying, but his temper was rising. Just in time, Michael saw what was happening but did not intervene, instead he went to the back of his Prado, opened the booth and handed over something to Desmond saying,

"Ol boy just give them this let them go!"

Desmond looked at it and smiled, pushing the nearest one to him away he poured the gin from the bottle Michael gave him onto the next thereby igniting the cigarette he had in his mouth so that his face was scalded in the process. As he was screaming the other brought out a small crude looking handgun and was moving closer to Desmond when Michael shouted at him, the cult boy turned round to stare into the hard-cold dark barrel of a Beretta AR70 assault rifle, on his other hand Michael carried a stick-tazer;

"You wan dance disco or you wan go get your 'odu'? Man me shebi you have a test tomorrow?"

As the boy turned back to face Desmond his cheek kissed the end of a Walther P99 pistol.

"You were saying son...?"

At this point students had taken to their heels deserting the whole place. The two remaining cultists were detained until the campus security came to take custody of them after Michael identified himself to them.

Fortunately, the boys couldn't make any connection to Sophia. Even if they did, word would go round quickly that Sophia and her clique were off-limits. The boys were much lower down the food chain, they were there to case the area for another rival gang's activities. If they had informed one of the higher ups, they would have been advised to steer clear, but they didn't.

They had failed in their mission, embarrassed them and broken ranks for some selfish desires; they would be punished severely for that.

On their way back to his hotel, Desmond knew it was time to tell Michael the real reason why he had come to Nigeria; about his father and the recent turn of events.

"My return to Nigeria after all these years was not just for holiday, I am on a job. I think my purpose and the recent turn of events can align for a mutual benefit."

"What are you saying Desmond? Tell you what, let me make a stop at that petrol station and we can talk for a bit in the car." Typical of the military boys, yet contrary to his style, Michael made a sudden turn from the inner lane to the outer lane earning some curses and invectives from other road users, but as they noticed his uniform, everyone quickly stifled their anger and sped off.

"First, you need to understand that my activity here has nothing to do with you and I don't want you to go into this without knowing the truth."

"Desmond, what are you talking about? Stop talking innuendos, spill it! Are you DMI?

Desmond cocked one eyebrow up giving him a strange stare. "I am not DMI and I am not CIA either; I am a defense contractor and carry out special tasks for the US government."

"You mean you are a mercenary, aren't you too young for that? Besides you are not French or Belgian or English, that's the specialty of their trigger happy dishonorably discharged soldiers! So, tell me are you here to destabilize the country? Or are you the cause of the the recent turmoil? Come on Desmond, what have you drawn us into?!"

"Hey, hey; brother, calm down. I am not here to cause civil strife, that's a different department. Actually, we don't want that because everyone in Europe and America as well as

Asia are afraid of the humanitarian crisis and that it could destabilize the equatorial region so they are keen to maintain some balance here rather than upset. However, they need this country to grow up and out of dictatorship because this is the only nation that can checkmate apartheid south Africa. But 'man me' that's not what I'm here for." Desmond gesticulated to Michael to calm down, also keeping an eye on his friend's hands peradventure he reaches for a weapon.

"Look brother, there's some information that was inadvertently left behind at the presidential palace. One of the general's guests is in possession of it and since she went in, one has seen or heard from her. I am here to retrieve it before it leaves the country or changes hands."

Michael's soldiers relaxed a little, but he was still clearly semi-cocked and he urged Desmond on. "Yes, go on, because I am seriously considering arresting you right now and I will drive you to DMI myself."

"My orders are to bring back the item, even if I have to bring the lady back dead or alive. The package must be returned to the US or worst case the consulate. I can use my resources to help with finding and rescuing Lance. However, I will need you to help me get closer and possibly into the presidential palace. I need to make this work so that my employers don't think I'm going off-track with my involvement in the Lance matter. You can see I am walking a tight rope. We'll make it look like I am still developing local assets."

"God punish you and your CIA gogon biris! Na me you wan take do asset?! Me Desmond?! I swear, if no be say you be my guy, I for don scatter ya head now - now! Do you know I am a decorated officer in the Nigerian Army?! Aaah!"

"Michael, I copy. For all it's worth, there is this guy I used to know in the States, we were in the marines together, he is very good at surveillance."

"What do you mean surveillance? For whom?"

Desmond smiled, "See, when investigating people, the police style, the investigator is exposed; but with espionage style he can only get information that is available for stealing but this guy he is what we call a 'pretender'. Like a bug he can get into any situation and do both." He was one of the two people ever to access the bedroom of the US President while he was sleeping and took a picture of him and his wife."

"How is that my business?"

Desmond made a different play. "If I mess this up Michael, how do you think it will help me find my father?"

It worked the magic.

"Okay so where do I come in? What is your plan?" Michael asked and Desmond responded. " I'm not sure yet but my target is the presidential villa.

"The rock? That's impossible!"

"Well, we'll see about that won't we Michael?"

Before dropping Desmond off, Michael asked Desmond a question. "Why didn't you offer me money to help you with your assignment or buy my cooperation and silence?"

Desmond replied. "I couldn't insult you with such an offer; I cannot put a price on your integrity or loyalty."

Desmond was let off at the main gate of his hotel at his insistence. He wanted to survey the place and be sure he wasn't being followed or watched. Upstairs in his room he sent out a message on the net; "My electrician I need some Naira quick."

CHAPTER 3

THE ELECTRICIAN

A janitor was mopping the floor of the University of Kumasi Senate lobby, just by the elevator lobby; his wristwatch started beeping. He was very dark skinned with graying hair especially at the sides, his dungarees did well to hide his well-muscled and trained body. To any of the other staff, and students he was just a harmless old cleaner who was very happy with his job and made everyone else around him happy. He dropped his mop and stepped into the empty lift; he understood Desmond's message clearly; only Desmond called him electrician and that naira meant Nigeria, also it was quick in the commercial capital. He pressed a button on his watch, he knew how to locate Desmond.

There was a knock on Desmond's door, it had been three days since he called for the electrician.

"Yeah who is it?"

"Room service, I brought your supper and a message from the electrician."

Desmond opened the door to a valet carrying his supper in a tray and for the benefit of eavesdroppers he said, "You can drop them on the dining…"

As he shut the door, they exchanged pleasantries and sat down to talk over supper.

In the belly of the rock under the presidential palace; one of the reasons why the general had personally supervised the design of the presidential villa; a dungeon where he kept most of his important enemies. Recently, due to his failing health he couldn't torture them himself, instead his chief security officer with his two sons took care of that for him.

Colonel Jia walked into the central corridor and was saluted by two guards, he didn't even take notice of them as he walked into the operating room where they dismembered the general's specimens, glancing inside he demanded for something and walked briskly away to another door which had a very bright red paint, as he stepped within fifteen centimeters the door swung open electronically controlled triggered by a weight sensor under the tile just in front of the door. On entering, the screams of some wild animal reached him form the interior and he spun on his heels to the door on his left, opened it and went down the stairs deeper into the belly of the blood fed rock where the screaming was even louder. It wasn't a wild animal but a dehumanized homo-sapiens of the nineteen nineties. Origin; Nigeria. He was in the nude with tiny dark spots of dried blood all over his body where the needle like electrodes had been pushed into his body not even his testicles had been spared. Jia did not wince at the sight, as far as he was concerned the man deserved it. Two of the men working on him stopped and turned round to face Jia.

"Who authorized this?!" He barked at them.

"Disconnect him now!"

No one moved, but a very young man not more than a boy was smiling and Jia knew who was responsible. He demanded for the most senior officer there, a sergeant stepped forward.

"I gave strict orders Sergeant, that on one should come in here without authorization either from me or the General," he turned to the youngster.

"More so, I am the only one to carry out this treatment on who I choose, but you have disobeyed me again. I swear, I will shoot you and I don't care if your father is the head of state!"

The boy stepped away from the controls and out of the room, with a rebellious cocking of his head, trying not to look humiliated.

In a solitary confinement cell in one of the maximum security prisons somewhere in the country, Lance lay on the floor of his cell it was like hell; a broken nose, damaged ear drums and swollen eyes that is to say that both eyes were swollen but the left eye was more and even shut, two of his fingers were broken; he wasn't even sure which, he couldn't feel the rest of his body; mosquitoes were having a party on him, but he was oblivious of that. He couldn't move anything. His body had gone into shock as a response to the pain and shutdown most of his motor-functions. He kept thinking of; what sin he had committed against God to warrant such suffering and what they had done to his private parts as a broomstick had been passed into it while he was questioned concerning the murder of his boss. He didn't even know the colonel had gone out let alone been killed in a car bombing until he was whisked from his office in the morning. Oh God! He thought and passed out again. That was the rhythm his body played in four days, slipping in and out of consciousness to help his mind and body heal. Later his captors would put him on a drip; that was how they kept him energized but impoverished.

Osmond looked almost okay except that his hearing was now defective as a result of the five dirty slaps he had received from his captors; the horsewhip lashes to his head and cuffs biting deep into his wrist and ankles.

They said, "Oga wants you very fit for the guest house!"

He couldn't really understand it all, first they told him a police officer had been looking for him and asking questions about his past, next thing SSS men burst into his office and arrest him accusing him of treason and being an American spy and trying to topple the government of the republic. For the second time in his life he became afraid for himself and muttered something under his breadth then called out to one of the guards. It took a while before anyone came.

"Please if you will, can I have my rosary, it is a prayer…,"

the prison guard interrupted him. "I bloody know what it is. Is that why you are calling for our commanding officer? Nonsense! Let me hear your noise again and I will kuku ma remove your teeth, useless berger!"

Just when he had given up hope the door opened and a plain-clothes man entered holding a novel in one hand and with the other extended with the rosary, Osmond took note that he used his right hand. As he was leaving the man turned round and crouched beside Osmond whispering. "Sir, please, ehn. Don't worry later when my C.O. has gone, I will come and remove the hand-cuffs."

Instantly he stood up and walked out. Osmond didn't say a word.

Lt. Colonel Benjamin Balogun was on an assignment to the War College for his commanding officer. On the return journey he had made a stopover at other military formations to see three of his friends. Their wives had sent him with letters to them at the same time he had short meetings with them and hinted that the direction of the wind might change soon, that meant they were to await a signal either form him or his god father, Major General Suleiman Ramat if things were to go wrong unless of course his god father who was the provost of the war college turned against him which would mean the end of the road. At times like these very few people trusted each other in the military. The Major General had refused to be involved with any rebellion or coup, that was his life-boat through all the various regimes he had worked under, he was a career soldier not a soldier of fortune he said. If the Major General were to fail him like his father did then he would just as well kill himself. His friends; Major Abubakar, Captain Umar and Sergeant Chukwudi all got his message clearly, things had gotten way out of hand and soon someone would have to say enough is enough, they were trained to be professional soldiers. One thing that gave Benjamin hope were the words of Major General Sule; the man had walked him to his car stopped halfway and spoke.

"Ben, whatever you do for the good of the nation you swore to serve and defend, don't be afraid to do it. I promise you, somewhere and somehow you will find good men who will stand by you, as sure as Allah lives!"

They saluted and he watched the old war horse walk back to his office block slapping his cane on his thigh. He didn't know what would really happen neither did he know who Desmond was but he was charismatic and could have passed off as a younger version of the Major General. Whatever the case may be the die had been cast. He drew out his side arm, released the safety lock and kept it on the seat beside him making sure to point the barrel towards the door as the army green Peugeot 504 salon car sped along the winding Ilorin expressway.

"Yes madam, I was a ship cook before I met the younger sister to my 'femer messer's' wife, bet…"

The heavy accent was beginning to give her a headache as she had to replay most of his words in her head to figure out what he was saying. Despite her own limited vocabulary in English, this guy made her feel like she spoke oxford English.

"It's alright!"

The woman cut him short; she was dark skinned, robust and with Tiv tribal marks. She was the charge d 'affairs of all the domestic staff and local dishes in the presidential villa, answerable only and directly to the first lady. She could well pass for the fifth most powerful and untouchable citizen in the country. The same man who had been janitor in Kumasi was now standing before her in the domestic staff laundry room the woman glanced at him again. He appeared to be all the Kwara state administrator's wife said he was except that she didn't mention he was so handsome. Any way one more hand to share in the national cake wouldn't hurt, more so she needed somebody to help her with her back ache. She was sure he could give a good massage with those hands of his and the muscles. He would get very good lodging.

"Are you ready now?"

He replied. "Bet yes madam; neu, neu."

"Okay, follow me."

Hajjiya definitely knew her taste very well, she thought to herself.

CHAPTER 4

MAY WEEK ONE

Apart from running out of them, Desmond didn't need any more excuses for going to see Sophia at her university. Sometimes he would go to her faculty and wait until her lectures were over. At the first few attempts she had scolded him, rebuked him, refused to see him, even at a point tried using one of her male colleagues to intimidate him; he had called the boy 'a champion without a trophy', her 'assistant boyfriend'. She also did remind him of her 'boyfriend' who had grown very curious about him. She liked Desmond a lot but it was messing with her head and she wasn't sure if the timing was right for her. At last she relaxed with him and accepted his invitations to take her out. Since he wasn't going to be in the country for long, soon she'd be free of his advances. She had insisted on not going for any late-night dates or dusk till dawn moves. A couple of times he would go with her to evening Mass at the school chapel, it turned out to be an inspiring experience for him specially to see that many university students still going to church. He didn't know how to be romantic the 'Unilag-culture Way', a few pointers from Ronke helped to fix things.

It had been a day of tactical planning with his new gang, after their 'operation rescue Lance' meeting he'd gone to visit Sophia; the errand boy; young expectedly harmless teenagers from the neighboring town act as runners for the student population. They typically hang around the female hostels from dusk till when the gates are shut to visitors. It was a good paying job and convenient too for all their patrons, from message exchanges to groceries and minor errands, it was a good industry. He was told that she had gone to see one of her friends in another hostel, he left her a message and got into his car. He'd just turned on the ignition, getting ready to back his car out of the lot when he felt a light, slight smack on his left ear lobe and he turned sharply thinking it was an insect, only to find Sophia standing there clutching a 'risky burger'.

"Hi Prince, going somewhere?"

"Err yes. No. Actually I just left you a message, oh never mind"

He turned off the engine and stepped out. Sophia was wearing a sleeveless light blue checkered shirt knotted above the navel on a sky-blue pair of comfort slim Wrangler Jeans and brown suede moccasins; sitting on the hood of his car.

"I thought you had started avoiding me again."

Sophia, feigning surprise, but with a mischievous smile on her face said. "Why would you think such?"

"Just a suspicion. Look I get it. You have a boyfriend, I am coming on strong, you have tons of school work. The gentleman in me wants to make it easy on you and walk away, but to be honest, I am too attracted to be that guy…. that's not to say I intend doing anything dishonorable."

"Yes, I get what you mean but seriously a lot is going on with me at the moment. You are also much older than I am and I will need some growing up time too. It's just crazy that I would normally have prevented things from getting to this point with you." She sighed. "There's no doubt about it, I do like you and find you very attractive but, don't you think we should play safe?"

"Play it safe? I don't understand…"

Suddenly they heard some noise from one of the dark spots near the entrance to the hall. Someone was getting beat up and of course, people started to run in anticipation of more violence. Sophia quickly explained to Desmond and was getting ready to bid him goodnight, she had to slap him lightly on the cheek to draw his attention from the spot.

"Desmond you have to go! Now!"

She got his attention and he could see she was really scared, though looking at her with a blank stare. Then with a very swift movement pulled her up close and planted his lips on hers. Maybe it was the swiftness of the movement, but for a split second she did not resist then suddenly she pushed him away and connected with a very sharp slap across his face, turned away and ran into her hostel. Desmond jumped into his car, revved the engine and with a squeal of tyres while muttering under his breath.

"This should even things up a bit."

With his head lights turned on full he drove straight into the brawling group as if to run them over but at the last moment he stopped so that the assailants had to abandon their victim and scattered away from the spot a short distance away and fired shots blindly in his direction, missing him and his vehicle. The headlights made it difficult for them to see or understand what was happening. Quickly he changed gears and reversed the car driving backwards for some distance across the avenue, then executed a spin with his hand brake and headed towards the campus gate. That was the break the boy being cudgeled needed and he made a run for it.

Konwe was asleep when he was rudely woken up by persistent banging on the door of their room. When he opened the door someone pushed him aside, slammed the door shut and turned off the lights. He stared hard at his uninvited guest from where he was lying on the floor before he realized or suspected it was his roommate Nduka. By this time the other roommates were awake. They all couldn't sleep a wink after he had narrated to them how some cult boys had brutalized him because they met him on the bed of one of their pal's girlfriend. If any of his roommates ever liked him before at that point, they all hated him for they were all marked targets because of him. They had warned him about the girl, but it fell on deaf ears.

The new servant man at the presidential palace, Ananse had a well-furnished servants' quarters with a television, video c.d. player, stereo set and apart from its own internal T.V. aerial it was connected to the villa's main satellite T.V system. This was a luxury reserved for only the staff supervisors or special undocumented guests that couldn't be kept in the main guest houses and needed to enjoy certain privileges.

He didn't find it difficult converting the TV aerial and a few other items into a mini encrypted radio communications system linking Desmond's laptop via satellite. Only Desmond's decoder could make meaning of any transmission either through his laptop or his cellphone. Only very few people could pull that off. Ananse had taken time to plant some of his monitoring devices in the palace; he planned to install some bugs tonight. In their line of work, everyone was an asset, even those who think you are their asset. Desmond was called the 'Engineer', he was good at creating opportunities, engineering options that were not there or no one else could see. Even though he was a free agent, he was still highly sought after. He, the electrician had other instructions that were in the cooler waiting for such an opportunity as the one Desmond had created. Desmond thought he was recovering a package but in truth he had just been harvested to give them access to Africa's most powerful and unpredictable dictator. He would go deeper into the palace and tag the private quarters and the 'rooms of interest'. First he had to get ready for his new madam, he helped her with her back ache; rummaging in the back of his bathroom cabinet he brought out a plastic bottle of pills, then he smiled.

They had well laid out plans. The intel was that both Lance and Chief Kobimdi had been transferred to a maximum-security prison in Bauchi and would soon be taken to the Rock. They were going to storm the Bauchi prison over the weekend. Everyone was expected to go on with their business as usual but on Saturday night they would all move into Emeka's flat at the senior air officer's barracks. Emeka had swopped his flying schedule with another pilot who needed to see his young wife at the Benin base so that on Sunday morning he would land his L-39 at the Benin base under a technical fault; switch to the chopper run with a Mil Mi-17 utility helicopter instead of his L-39 Albatross. The others would meetup with him traveling by road at the rendezvous point. There was a radar blind-spot where he would land and pick them up, no one would know he had put the bird to ground. Pick up some cargo for drop off at Enugu, refuel and make a quick detour to Bauchi. They had to make it a quick landing at Bauchi, hit and run under cover of night, then make a quick refueling stop at the Kaduna airbase and back to Benin for the switch back to Lagos. Hopefully the fault is not fixed until he suggests a solution to the engineers on Monday morning to catch the end of his schedule so that he would be seen in his Albatross landing in Lagos after a harrowing experience. The rescue team would do a road trip back to Lagos with a plan B to head towards Calabar for a border crossing to Cameroun if necessary. The key was to get the duo out of harm into safety. Their days in the country was over, for the time being.

Michael had been going over the plans in his head when he turned into his street. There was an army truck parked in front of his house with no one around except the driver who was wearing combat fatigues with camouflage bush cover on his helmet. This was typically worn for drills or real combat situations including counter-insurgency operations. They are not typical for house calls and besides if he was being redeployed or summoned, a signal would not come like this unless there was trouble.

Michael pulled out his side arm and kept it in the vacant slot under his car stereo; then calmly slotted in a cassette that had finished playing into the car stereo. He tapped his horn to announce his arrival and the gate was opened. As he drove into the compound, his sentry saluted him and he noticed the Privates boots were off. His stomach tightened, he knew the sentry always relaxed when he was gone for work but just before he came back the Private would dress properly. From the corner of his eye he saw his friend, Lieutenant Felix Amokpai come out from the front, saluted him then went to Michael's side of the car.

"Colonel, there has been a problem. Desmond has been killed we don't know who or why but SuPol Joseph said I should locate you immediately, so I came here straight with extra security,"

There was distress written all over his face and for a brief moment Michael too was lost then he asked. "When did this happen? Where is he now, I mean Desmond?"

"Sir, he has been moved to the hospital near his hotel, he is in intensive care unit, it's a private clinic, the SuPol said to take you there once I get you. The cassette ejected and Michael cursed the stereo just loud enough for Lt Felix to hear and made as if to turn it off. As he reached for his gun, he noticed the silhouette of soldiers in the guard house, and fired through the door at Felix. The car was still running and he had clutched and braked at same time, so he just accelerated into his house smashing through the front porch into his sitting room. It wasn't clear who was more surprised by the action – himself or the other soldiers hiding in the corner. The confusion that created bought him the precious few seconds he needed.

Michael was bleeding all over his face from several cuts, he reached for his glove compartment and brought out a piece of rag and two hand grenades; he wiped his face with. Then kicked out his door and fell out of the Prado He ran through the partially demolished sitting room to the kitchen and threw himself at the door leading to the back of his house, removed the lid of the septic tank and from some hidden cavity he pulled out a large and heavy army ruck sack, threw it over his fence then followed it. He unplugged one of the grenades and threw it over his fence back into his house; the explosion not only rocked the entire estate but also got all his neighbors scampering for cover and shutting themselves up in their homes. In the compound he jumped into there were six cars parked there, all in good shape, he knew the family very well, reaching for the nearest one that had its windows wound down. It was an estate and he quickly broke into the ignition after dumping his load in the back and backed the car out in a hurry taking down the gate in the process.

The years Desmond had spent working for the Pentagon and NATO as a Marine Raider with the Special Operations Forces (SOF) and the NATO Response Force (NRF) improved his sense of caution, thanks to modern technology, he had provided and insisted all his close friends carry pagers on them for as long as they were involved in the mission. Barrister Gerald and SP Jojo were told to stay behind the scene and be their emergency escape facilitators. Neither Lt Azuka nor Lt. Col. Benjamin knew this. They both assumed that the duo had been removed from the plan because they were too high profile.

As the metallic blue station-wagon car raced along the rail lines heading towards the air base at Oshodi, five pagers were beeping continuously in different parts of the city.

Navy Captain Francis Otoluwa, Frank, was on leave; after his last deployment with ECOMOG forces in Liberia he had been redeployed to another fleet and put on six weeks leave until his reassignment. He was just replacing his golfing kit in the back of his Prado when his paging device went off beeping all over, he unclipped it from his shorts and was about to turn it off but thought better of it, the message could only mean trouble. He didn't even remember to shut the hatch door instead he clambered into the driver's seat through the open back and kicked the car to life. The parking lot was sparsely occupied so that instead of reversing over and over he made a swift turn and as if hell had been let loose gunned the car out of the club gates. As soon as he entered the road he sighted far off a military truck with combat dressed soldiers carrying guns in the back, he turned off sharply into Kingsway road and sped off. The truck was flashing it's headlights at Frank as he got stuck in a heavy traffic popularly called 'go-slow', soldiers started jumping down from the truck running towards him, he opened his door then changed his mind, the traffic opposite him was free, he turned his Prado, went over the culvert and sped towards the bridge on the driving against normal traffic flow, with his full lights on he thundered up the road and onto the bridge. Lagosian road users were quick to adjust to him since, it had become normal for such stunts to be pulled by the military boys.

Frank suddenly realized that there were no more vehicles coming towards him, though the army truck was still on his tail. At the top of the bridge he found out why.

A road block had been set up using a much bigger army truck and they were waiting for him; he had been cornered. They opened fire on sighting him; he got hit twice so that he swerved losing control of the car and ran into the bridge railing. His safety belt and airbags had prevented him from flying through the wind screen. Quickly he disengaged himself, the door had been flung open by the impact so he rolled out, climbed over the railing and was about to jump when a bullet hit him throwing him far into the water.

Lt Colonel Balogun was just coming out of his office block on his way to the senior officers' mess when a military truck pulled up short at the beginning of the stone pavement near his car. One of his lieutenants came out and joined him. He was still staring at the truck when two army officers alighted and walked briskly towards him. One was a sergeant carrying an AK-47 while the other was a Major.

As they got closer, they didn't salute him, the major spoke first and with authority.

"Lt Colonel Benjamin Balogun? I have come to relieve you of your post and place you under arrest!"

The first lieutenant retorted

"Major! You are talking to a superior officer?!"

Ignoring him the major continued to command the sergeant to remove Ben's sidearm, muttering.

"I don't have time to waste."

The lieutenant pushed Ben's sidearm back in its holster and stood between them and Ben shouting, "Brigade under attack, all men fall in and fire at will!"

He took the Ak and first shot in the air then aimed at the sergeant's leg. The soldiers in the back of the truck were taken unawares. They thought it would be an easy take like other arrests. The first two to recover quickly jumped down and started to fire at Ben and his Lt. they both had the element of surprise and capitalized on it to quickly duck behind one of the office walls. By now Ben had pulled out his own service pistol and started to exchange fire with all the soldiers. Soon other officers and NCOs came rushing to the scene and a shoot-out ensued. Not many understood what was happening but they were aware that somehow the truck and its occupants were a threat to their Lt Colonel Ben which meant they were all at risk until they figure out where the threat was coming from. More than anything else, they were fighting for their own skin. Clearly these guys were not from the Cantonment, they were outsiders and unless their GOC came out to call for a cease fire, they would keep shooting at the aggressors. They were fighting for everything that represented their chain of command and for themselves and that was a good enough reason to open fire at all the soldiers it spewed forth. Suddenly a grenade hit the truck and the shooting ceased with the explosion. Ben had been hit and was down, quickly he was rushed into his car enroute to the hospital. On their way to the military hospital, Ben opened his eyes and beckoned for his aide-de-camp to come closer gave him a piece of paper pointing repeatedly at it then passed out, he was bleeding from a head wound.

The court was a state high court, it was still the old colonial building that was once the colonial governor's. Not a whole lot had changed, it was not built to have any air-conditioning, back then it was just a ceiling fan. After the independence in 1960, not much was changed – besides the military dictatorships had very little regard for civil law so there was no investment in that area. For some buildings window units were retrofitted into the old sturdy structures, for some nothing was done, simply to ensure that those who didn't have would be reminded of their place in society; air-conditioning was for those who mattered. The court room was still the same small townhall type of arrangement meant to humiliate the Africans, typical of the colonialists and escort them through mostly rehearsed show of false justice and a speedy trial to punishment. It was built to be uncomfortable so that Judge, Jurors and Jury would be in a hurry to finish the business and get out of the building. Coupled with the almost non-existent public utility power – it was clearly not the place to seek justice. The accuser would typically be frustrated unless it were the military federal government. Gerald was sweating profusely, he had been at the court all day with his client, there was a power failure and the Judge had called for a recess until power was restored. They weren't ready to buy diesel for the court house generator again like they did on previous court sittings for the past two months so they would wait for the power authority to do their work today.

He had unbuttoned his shirt and taken off his wig when the pager started beeping. All he muttered to his client was, "Sir, I'm sorry, i have to go now, an emergency!"

He entered his car and left.

The state administrator's wife was still in a bad state. She had witnessed the whole thing. They had fought that morning because of his womanizing and philandering, she had insisted on going with him for the impromptu meeting – she had accused him of going to see his mistress. He wasn't a violent man, which was interesting for such a powerful man. He had calmly removed her from himself and begged her to stay home that it was a security meeting he was going for. She had refused until he asked one of his sentries to take her indoors. He had saved her life.

Security had been beefed up around her with soldiers all over the house after the car bombing of her husband. The police had been posted along the streets and estate. Police Superintendent John Joseph was one of the officers from the Lagos State Police command drafted there in conjunction with the 'Operation Sweep Squad'; a special joint taskforce set up by the late Administrator in response to the terrible crime rate in the state. It had succeeded to drop crime rate, especially violent crimes by 70% in six months. He'd quickly become a state hero for that singular achievement, so his death was a severe blow to Lagosians. SP Jojo was discussing with his colleagues out of boredom and some of them knew it was the 'General' who masterminded the killing of the administrator either directly or otherwise. It was even more disturbing since the culprits they were supposed to be looking out for were their bosses, but no one dared speak their mind. Suddenly everyone there even Jojo was startled by a beeping sound. This was strange as it was unlike their walkie-talkies which crackled rather than beeped, someone said something about a bomb and they all froze crouching as if they could escape if indeed it was a bomb. A sudden realization made Jojo to jump, he reached for the nearest squad car and took off with it. No one was surprised for they all knew Jojo as the 'hot stuff action man', probably he was on another special assignment and summoned by the 'powers that be' or something.

Squadron Leader Emeka Uboni had just dumped two heavy duffel bags and a few ruck sacks into his car when a metallic blue Mercedes Benz estate screeched to a halt beside him, he swore under his breath then saw Michael's head.

"Ol boy quick, don't use your car, there is trouble."

Without asking questions they loaded all the sacks into the Mercedes and drove off. Emeka's beeper had been on time.

Since the night he kissed Sophia, things had gone bad between them. The last time they spoke, she had simply said, "You once told me you'd do that and you went ahead and did it. So, I'm going to be tough on you this time."

Then she turned and walked back into her faculty. He didn't expect that response to the kiss; and he beat himself up about it. Looking back, he wasn't sure what compelled him to make such a move on Sophia. For several days before that evening, she had been on his mind to a point of obsession and much as he tried to fight it, he couldn't. He also thought about kissing her a lot – probably he let that animal in and it became a monster that consumed him. After the last time she dismissed him, she would see him and just ignore him, she's always busy; her friends would decline any request for assistance claiming that she was so busy and they hardly saw her around. He had refused to let his cousin get involved, even though the boy knew about it; students talk and news like that always travels through different channels but, he wasn't going to get Konwe involved. At some point he had become quite upset with Sophia and once thought she was being childish and immature. The next day he would become remorseful and long for her again. On the other hand, he knew she was a distraction to his mission; she was an unplanned variable, was it a good thing to let her be a factor in his world at this time? Ronke finally gave him some useful information, that Sophia's boyfriend had gotten wind of their 'not so secret' affair and became more persistent with her trying to get her back. It had all become too much for Sophia who decided to get herself some space, so Sophia had moved back home. There was no talk about 'the kiss'; though, the new information gave him some comfort, on the other hand, her not telling anyone about 'the kiss' made him even more uncomfortable. Ronke had reached out to him that Sophia had a late seminar and would be spending the night in school. He had to try and iron things out with her.

Desmond parked his Volvo in front of the New-Hall complex for male students. Locked up then as he walked away turned on the anti-theft alarm.

Upstairs he met his cousin Konwe, after they'd talked for a while he stood up to go, he told Konwe he wanted to see Sophia but he would rather walk down. Konwe really appreciated the occasional visits of his cousin not only for the financial benefits but it made him feel some important relation had not forgotten him and a role model at that. So, he was willing to walk Desmond almost all the way but Desmond declined saying,

"No, I met you studying, go back to your books. Maybe over the weekend both of us will hangout, if you like with some of your friends or just us. Ok?"

Konwe understood, sometimes his cousin reminded him of 'batman'.

Konwe and Desmond used different stairways for an adjacent wing downwards. Outside he just meandered through the crowd of students in an attempt to not stand-out or draw attention. Desmond had just reached the Mass-Communications departmental building when his pager started beeping, immediately he turned around and started running back the way he had come.

When Konwe got back to his room there were three men waiting there for him. They wore suits and Kingsley, his roommate had been attending to them. As he entered the room Konwe joined Kingsley on the table closest to the window as he was questioned about the whereabouts of his visitor. The two boys, though scared, asked the men to identify themselves, instead one of the men produced a gun and demanded for Desmond declaring that they were SSS officers; expecting the gun would reinforce clear the air about their intentions. It caused the desired effect as the boys started saying so many things at the same time, in tears saying they had no idea their visitor was a fraudster, that they were not in on his deals. For a moment the security men became confused and ordered them to shut up. They heard some shouting down the hall and foot falls of running people one of the security men opened the door and peeped outside, at that moment Nduka burst into the room, he was bleeding from the side of his head. He blurted out, "Kingsley! Konwe! Help! They are going to kill me, those boys again…"

Followed by gun shots, with the new entrant, the SSS men became distracted turning their attention to the door and all the pandemonium. That was all the time the youngsters needed. In that moment Kingsley grabbed Konwe from behind and threw both of them out through the window tearing the mosquito netting and smashing the glass with his back in the process.

The door came down and the SSS men opened fire. After the shooting died down no one was standing in the room.

Konwe and Kingsley fell to the ground-floor and landed on a heap of laundry which the laundry workers had gathered to do, picking themselves up they stumbled towards the service entrance of their hostel. The shooting had triggered a stampede which wasn't unusual, within minutes the whole chaos would die-down as if nothing happened. Only those directly involved would carry the scars and the knowledge fir the rest of their lives.

Outside in the parking lot two of the cult students who had been beating up Konwe's friend Nduka, the other night had recognized Desmond's car and started vandalizing it, smashing the windshield behind, the other two SS officers waiting in their station wagon 504 car intervened opening fire on the two kids. Other members of their gang attacked the SS men drawing them away from their car.

Desmond was running down from the New-hall gate when he met the stampede of students running for cover. He got through to his car, saw his cousin and someone else stumbling towards him. Desmond instinctively slid over the hood and ran to them. He caught up with them and together with Konwe dragged his friend, Kingsley to the car. As soon as they got into the car, Desmond got the car out of the area and sped off. Konwe crying and painting still bewildered asked his cousin, "Uncle, why were SSS men looking for you?"

Desmond just stared at him in his rear-view mirror then shook his head without saying a word.

CHAPTER 4

MAY WEEK FOUR

Pro-Democracy movements and Student Unions were whipping up sentiments, and demanding for the release of all political prisoners especially the latest two; Lawrence Ayinde and Chief K.O. Bindi. Pockets of riots had been experienced in different parts of the country. At the same time, Professor Richard Balogun who was campaigning for the self-succession bid of the head of state had been placed on house arrest following his son's involvement with Desmond's group.

At the presidential villa, Colonel Jia had Chief Osmond Kobimdi and Lawrence brought before him.

"I know your foreign sponsors sent a team of mercenaries to come and save you. They were foolish and we have killed them. The others, we will hunt them down soon and for your information we will execute you both on the anniversary of our regime that is the first week of next month, I'd like to see them rescue you here."

He was a soft-spoken soldier, there were rumors that his voice sounded feminine as such no one took him seriously. In order to save face, the army had posted him to the intelligence unit where it was discovered that he lacked the aptitude required for analysis and strategy, but they discovered he had a thing for forcing information out of people. He was left there and abandoned until the 'General' discovered him and started mentoring him.

Col Jia gestured for them to be returned to their cells. Lance's condition had improved from near death to very bad, apart from the whipping and electrocution they administered on him and Osmond, the indiscriminate beating had stooped. Osmond was the worse for it, an old man, he had become very nervous and tense after his third round on the electrocution bed. Sometimes they would just pour water on his naked body and apply an energized power cable on his wet body.

Somewhere in Lagos; one of those high-brow neighborhoods where fraudsters, drug traffickers, hitmen had formed a colony, bought property and developed. It was so because they enjoyed the protection of members of the junta, even though "drug peddling" was a crime punishable by death sentence or at best life imprisonment. Here everyone knew to mind their business, so it didn't draw any attention when a vacant duplex with its own compound and not so exquisite landscaping suddenly became full of nocturnal activity with windscreen smashed cars coming in and people sneaking out. This was the hideout where Desmond and his motley crew of co-conspirators had taken refuge. It was Michael's preparation for his retirement – which meant a bullet to the head. No one but his mother knew about it. He had money, travel papers and weapons buried at marked points; he had given his mother and siblings very clear instructions on what to do if he was ever arrested or killed. Desmond was part of that plan and his will executor. Only that Desmond wasn't aware of it.

They had all somehow, within three days of the attempted arrests made it there. Each, scared, though not showing it, no-one was sure of where the leak had come from. Apart from Benjamin the only other suspect was Emeka's brother Azu, but no one had seen or heard from him yet.

Emeka was livid with anger and had sworn to put a ARM through him whenever he saw him, which was an exaggeration of course, since an ARM is not a 'personnel calibre' type ordinance it was for big targets either ATS, ATA, STS or STA. ARMs are expensive and unless he was in a car, tank or strapped to a station large surface area object, Azu wouldn't be waiting to be fired at.

They were all gathered round a table, all the house light bulbs had been removed all they had were improvised field lamps made out of glowstick fluids. First, they lit the glow sticks, then cut off one end of each stick and emptied their contents into empty marmalade glass jars and mixed them with a universal solvent, screwed the lids back on, shook them to get dim but functional lighting. Of course the power outlets were still functional for electric powered non-illuminating appliances. Seated around the table were Colonel Benjamin Balogun, Navy Captain Frank, Lieutenant Colonel Michael, Squadron leader Emeka; SP John; Barrister Gerald and Desmond.

Ben had been wearing a Kevlar bullet proof vest when he was shot, but he had a deep cut on his temple; the bullet had grazed him with a flesh wound but slicing from the front to the rear – he would have a long scar like a parting for the rest of his life unless he wore a cap it would always be visible if he cropped his hair. His left arm was in a sling but he was still in good fighting condition. He had kept his lieutenant and driver a corporal with him and apart from their loyalty which he knew was unquestionably to him, he had promised to put a bullet in the head of any betrayer. Both were keeping watch from the windows at the top floor. Michael had several cuts all over his face from his windscreen but they were minor ones.

Frank had lost his left trigger-finger, had a broken nose and a lacerated calf, yet his fighting spirit was not dented. Frank also known as 'the fish' had managed to break out of his car after it hit the lagoon, swam underwater to one of the central pillars of the bridge then latched onto a ferry that was sailing past . It was a bumpy ride but it kept him alive and got him to safety.

Konwe and Desmond had taken Kingsley to a private hospital, the money Desmond paid to them was enough to buy their silence and provide Kingsley good care and a short stay. They would discharge him the next day and take him home with a cab; the nurse was well taken care of for that. Besides, they were not unfamiliar with University students coming in for such injuries like matchet cuts and bullet wounds, after all they get elite patients the staff nurse had said. Konwe had become their errand boy, going out at night to buy them food and other items. At first the boy was bewildered but when he recalled the story his mother had told him once about Desmond, he quickly got over it and applied himself to the responsibility which the situation offered.

By now the police were looking for Konwe and Kingsley but weren't sure of Desmond's identity. They were wanted in connection with the murder of five SSS officers in cold blood. Unfortunately, this had made them local heroes on campus.

At home Konwe's mother was in bad shape, the police had been there, SSS men too; questioning her about her son and nephew. The whole family was in great distress.

Desmond cleared his throat and everyone looked up, the air was thick with cigarette smoke, the scene reminded him of an old operation he was involved in that went bad; it started out as a rendition of a drug baron, then turned it a hit. His team had been getting their weapons ready; they were dressed like regular street guys so as to make it look like a rival gang hit. They never made it out of the safehouse because the Columbian police at least that was what they dressed like had swooped on them and killed everyone except him. He was barely alive with six bullet wounds on his body when the recovery team had found him. They put him in a Solitary Recuperation Programme (SRP) up in Nebraska for seven months for only one reason; he was their black box. He quickly blocked out the memory and he wiped off a tear, he had lost the first woman he'd ever allowed himself the luxury of loving that night, but that was then this is now.

Gerald asked, "Are you ok yellow?"

Desmond nodded, cleared his throat again.

"Gentlemen, brothers, we are in a bad situation, but not without hope. we cannot allow ourselves to become trapped by this tyranny. this has been an unprovoked and premeditated aggression against us. Make no mistake; its either we die or we survive and if we intend to survive, it is certain that things, can only get worse and will whether we do something or not. The general wants our heads served on his table, I say why don't we take the fight to him and have him for breakfast instead."

Ben spoke up, "What do you mean?"

Michael opened his mouth to say something but did not. Did that the second time and on the third, by now having everyone turning to him he said. "OK, he wants us dead. I don't know why, all we wanted was to have our friend back. Well, now he has murdered sleep and he too will not sleep! I say we take him out!"

Some of the others shifted on their seats then Frank asked, "And after we take him out, what happens to his government, or we just take our friends out and leave the nation in confusion, haba! Yellow, won't you stop this madness?"

Before Desmond could respond, Ben raised his hand and spoke.

"We can take over the government, at least for some months until we find a suitable group of civilians who can…"

Ben didn't finish before an argument ensued on this. Desmond wanted to shout, but thought better of it instead he covered the lamp with a bandana plunging the dimly lit room into darkness which silenced everyone, then he removed it again restoring illumination only to see guns drawn.

"No put away your weapons, I only wanted your attention. I think you guys have a point; Ben you are right we will need to take control at least to forestall an unhealthy power tussle. This will be for as long as it takes to establish an interim government. I however, cannot be part of such because I am not here as a Nigerian and the upheaval will not be pleasing to my home country. I could even be arrested for several different international crimes. Remember when we toasted to a civilian coup, then it was a joke, now it is real."

Michael raised his hand speaking at the same time without waiting for permission, "Excuse me your outlaw-ness but, how precisely are we to take over from the presidential guards, look my friend that place is a fortress, they are programmed to keep shooting at anything and anyone who tries anything until the last bullet, even…"

Ben interrupted him.

"I promise you will not be fighting alone, I already put some of my people in the presidential guards on the alert. They are silent friends who are also tired of the killings and the mess the military has become. I assure you that within minutes of the signal, the gates of the rock will be down, but see there are three ways in; through the gate and get blown off by the anti-tank guns, through the perimeter fencings and either be mowed down by snipers or blown-up by land mines, or getting in from the air, it's no secret that the villa's airspace is a restricted zone to unauthorized flights that means anti-aircraft missiles with tracers.

Again, everyone went quiet.,

"Ehmm. Excuse me sir … "

It was Ben's lieutenant, getting a nod from Ben he went on.

"I have been with the presidential guards before redeployment, that was after the head of state had just moved in, we were put through the general plan of the place by the contractors, I think I know how we can get in."

Drawing sheets were produced and lieutenant Kukah went ahead to draw a sketch of the palace's layout from memory and explained how they could get in from one of the perimeter maintenance and utility tunnels.

Desmond had gone first to his hotel after he got Konwe and his friend to a hospital, his valet had been very cooperative; the boy had taken him up to his room through the kitchen and up the utility elevator they used for room service deliveries, then helped him carry his things through the same elevator down through the back door to his car.

Most of his things were still packed but the laptop, cellphone were set-up in his new room. At about one in the morning on Saturday they had drawn up details of how to break into the Rock.

When they had finished Desmond spoke, "We need to get some prominent pro-democracy people to constitute this constitute this congress…"

Jojo interjected,

"Interim government you mean."

"Yeah, whatever." Responded Desmond.

Emeka speaking for the first time said, "How do we do that?"

Desmond replied, "We abduct them, then brief them and swear them in!"

Jojo spoke again, "That is easy I know the residences of quite a number of them here in Lagos but we need a tight logistics setup."

At this point Ben's orderly and chauffer said he could get a military bus and drive it, everyone nodded their approval

It was 05:00 hours, Saturday morning and they were still busy drawing up names and dividing the country into six zones so that they got twelve nominees two from each zone, eight men and four women. All in an attempt to make it a balanced national group and avoid portraying the change as a regional or ethnic agenda.

While the others had gone to sleep, Desmond took out an envelope he saw slipped under his hotel room door when he had gone to get his things from the hotel. He opened it; it contained a card form Sophia, a very interesting poem was written but what really caught his attention was the message in tiny hand writing which said

"I'm sorry about the last time we saw and all the drama since, you know I don't like plain vanilla, I told you, next time make it strawberry P.S.I love you- Sophia"

It didn't make sense to him and was about to fling it way when he remembered he had sent her a bucket of Walls Ice-cream. He assumed it never made it to her or she had turned it down. It was vanilla flavored. He laughed, threw himself on the bed and dozed off.

On Monday morning the newspaper headlines screamed "MYSTERIOUS ABDUCTIONS!"; "PRO DEMOCRACY ACTIVISTS DISAPPEAR!" another read, "SIXTEEN ELDER STATESMEN AND WOMEN MISSING!"

At the Presidential Palace there was confusion, the general had called Jia and was praising him for the initiative to deal with his enemies. Later, alone colonel Jia swore he would find out who had done it, for he knew this would cause more trouble than good if indeed it was true, and if it was his men, then who gave them the authorization? He thought maybe it was the insufferable son of the general? He would have to question him about it later.

Details of the events in Konwe's dormitory room had spread like wildfire, which was typical. Sophia wasn't spared the details either, although no one really knew what or how Desmond fit into the story, Sophia had drawn her own conclusions after Ronke confirmed her fears by telling her what she saw at Michael's place.

Sophia also concluded Desmond was dead and like two widows, they consoled each other holding each other in a long embrace and sobbing. Both decided it was best to move out of campus and back home for a while. Sophia being who she was, narrated her story to her parents. That night she cried till dawn, sometimes tears can rise up to heaven faster than a thousand words.

They had split themselves into three groups, it was quite easy for Ben's orderly to get an army bus. Desmond stayed with the bus and driver while the others went out into the city to get their targets. Some of their quarry were submissive, few scared stiff others who were constant callers at the SSS guard rooms insisted on telling their families but, Emeka wouldn't have any of that and had to knock them unconscious. While they were moving their captives into the bus most of them knew they would be probably shot somewhere because of the cloak and dagger style; a pair of eyes watched them from a parked army green Peugeot 504 sedan. The owner of the eyes also took care of the soldiers at a checkpoint just before Desmond and his team came through. He had been watching their house keenly for some time after they had been declared wanted by the DMI, Directorate for Military Intelligence and the State Security Service SSS.

Ananse knew about the General's orgies, of how he made arrangements for young ladies to be in his guest house. On two occasions, he had been one of those who attended to the guest house. An idea came up in his head and he smiled. The woman beside him stirred then asked him why he was smiling he answered with a lie which made her feel really good with herself.

CHAPTER 5

THE NIGHT IS DARKEST BEFORE DAWN

Sundays at the Muritala Mohammed International Airport weren't busy days. Very few flights came in and even fewer went out.

It was a little after midnight with rain pouring down as a storm, no one in their right mind would want to be caught in such downpour at night; so, most of the streets and roads were deserted. Desmond got out of bed and went round waking the others up

"Let's roll men!"

Without question they each jumped out of their makeshift beds, quickly and methodically gathered their things; guns, money, tools, knives, explosives and other sorts. There was no time for a bath, they were dressed in what they slept in dark camouflage fatigues and boots.

They gathered their captives and headed for the airport in the night downpour, the nationwide power outage gave them the perfect cover of darkness to travel to the airport unnoticed.

For Oshozie Sunday night shifts were very boring on the control tower, most of the time he would occupy himself with banter between him and some of the army privates usually assigned to the tower or play card games with them while they were still sober.

Tonight, as if as if it was not boring enough, it was raining which made him feel very sleepy despite the cold. The air-conditioning was one of the equipment they made sure was new and in tip-top shape to protect the control tower equipment from heating up and getting damaged, the runway lights too; but they had different backup power generators. With the control tower temperatures always kept at 18 degrees Celsius, the personnel on duty always had to wear thick jackets that made one feel very cozy at night and unless you had 'bitter kola' or inhumanely strong coffee, you'd still struggle to stay awake during the long 'graveyard shift'. Due to the notoriety of the country's unsafe air traffic control; night time flights were few and far in-between.

The lone soldier assigned on guard duty to the tower that night was already asleep on the bench in the corner. The soldiers had no idea what the air-traffic controllers (ATC) did; after the initial awe when they were newly assigned those duties, they just remained at their duty post until they start to relax and take off their uniforms one piece at a time; no one came to inspect at night, besides the airport duty was like a diplomatic mission - a smart soldier would make a good fortune from travelers in tips and gifts.

He glanced at the young private, he wasn't going to wake him; Oshozie placed his own feet on his desk set his earphones over his head, took one last look across the set of screens before him then closed his eyes and slept off; in this weather only a madman would be in the air he thought to himself.

Suddenly, the lights went off all over the airport. It was a blackout from the public utility supply. It would take at least thirty minutes to an hour before the backup generators would be turned on. It was not unusual. In the darkness a bus pulled up beside a Beechcraft 1990 King Air 350 belonging to one of the local airlines. The plane was bound for the Federal Capital but with the change in weather it had been delayed for over five hours running till that particular moment. The pilot and his crew were about to call it a night when, he heard some noise outside, as he stepped out into the main hangar to check on his plane, he got a Glock in his mouth instead.

Desmond was very charming and persuasive as he told the crew they were taking over the flight on a national assignment and asked them to treat their passengers and unwilling cargo to a wonderful time in the air. The pilot had been chloroformed into one corner while Emeka and the co-pilot took over. At first Emeka wasn't very sure but he quickly adjusted to the Beechcraft.

Oshozie had fallen off his chair when the crackle of words jarred him out of sleep. He quickly picked himself up and made out that he was being asked for clearance to take off. This he refused but, was taken aback when the voice threatened hm as an interfere in an official assignment from the presidency, the soldier who had woken up too, advised him to comply so that he doesn't book a ticket for the two of them to some military detention cell,

"If they want to kill themselves, please let them, it is not our business, look soldier work is; Soldier! If they say enter, obey before complain."

Even before Oshozie gave the clearance, he could see the silhouette of a small plane already gaining speed for take-off on the runway. He was a bit confused, the back-up generators were on, as he still struggled to gather his thoughts, he just mumbled a, "clearrrred….".

He had heard rumors of clandestine movements and flights but he'd never had any on his shift – the rule was 'see nothing, say nothing'. He was not obliged to document it; he didn't even know the call-sign. Someone had switched off the flight beacon.

Everyone in the plane was scared; no one flies in this kind of weather, but Emeka knew if there was anybody who could fly a plane even over a volcanic eruption it was a Nigerian air force pilot, to him it was a piece for cake! It took a similar threat to get the necessary landing permit at the Nnamdi Azkiwe International airports FCT. The air traffic controllers on duty were used to such bullying tactics anyway.

One thing this country's military juntas had become well known for was the habit of abandoning projects. Some of the buses used during the Pope's visit had been abandoned beside one of the unused hangers. It was an opportunity they shamelessly used to embezzle as much as they could and awarding to themselves the contract to buy them A lot of people did not fully understand the import of the warning of the Pope to the General to "let my people go". It was rumored that he cried when he was leaving the country and refused to use the vehicles provided for him as being like Moses being offered a ride on the back of the children of God by Pharaoh.

Ben knew this and as soon as they taxied to a stop, he got his orderly to follow him to get one and refuel it from one of the airport pumps. The rain was a very good cover like a silver curtain so that even the sentries and all posted around the airfield and airport were oblivious of the happenings. Ben remembered also some of the buildings that the General had scattered in the city that were not occupied but guarded by only two sentries or none at all. They got to one and it was not difficult to subdue the only guard stationed there, they were caught napping. Within minutes one of their loyalists had reported there on a motorcycle and took over guard duty.

Ben's lieutenant was a promising young officer, had a photographic memory and he quickly located the camouflaged area of the maintenance manhole seven kilometer from the primary perimeter fence of the rock. Two hours later the rain had stopped, they were still trying to get past the second door which was two kilometers from their target.

They had to wait till nightfall to breach.

The tunnel led them into a courtyard with what looked like a maze garden; it was floodlit making it impossible to cross without being noticed. They had to crawl on their bellies through the maze to mask their bodies from the lights until they got to the nearest building which looked like a disused sentry post attached to that building. It had a door and as they breached the lock and made their way inside, it led them down a stairway underground again to what they thought was a basement but turned out to be another tunnel running below the palace.

Lieutenant Kukah confirmed their position to be the presidential guest house wing of the palace. Doing a room-to-room or building to building search was out of the question they headed for the security post.

Major Usman Ezenuwa was a professional soldier stationed with the presidential guards; nothing had prepared him for the kind of security job he was posted to handle on this particular night. He was already disillusioned with his army career after 12 months as a major simply because the General wanted a security guard of officer cadre to help him keep his wife in check. The first day he reported with his signal to the commander, the man didn't even look at the signal, he simply threw it into his desk drawer and told him he had 2 simple jobs – the first to protect the life of the First Lady with his own; the second was ensure the head of state's wife can never catch him with his pants down. He'd served 3 tours on ECOMOG, he loved the action and his men; then they told him the high command was very impressed with his accomplishments after a visit from the theater commander and the head of state. He thought he was on a good run when they promoted him sooner than expected. Barely 2 years as a Captain. Here he was, withdrawn from the war front on ECOMOG duties where real fighting men should be; here he was a watchdog for adultery, a national filth. The stories he had heard about the presidential guards being an elite force... he hadn't seen anything to support that. They were all feeding fat and there was such indiscipline and lack of professionalism. They seemed to be more of shameless company of looters and debauchers rather than soldiers.

Suddenly he heard a scuffle behind him, he turned abruptly and got a gun in his face. Instinctively he kicked it off and at same time tried to pull out his knife; but Desmond was faster with a kick to his midsection which slammed his head on a desk as he hit the floor.

When he came to Michael questioned him about the two latest guests they had in the villa. Major Usman answered,

"My orders are to guard the head of state not to be prison warder, that is the priority of Special Forces! I don't know anything about guests or visitors or prisoners!"

Ben pushed Michael aside and pulled off his mask saying

"You seem to be doing a terrible job of it soldier….!"

"Whaat! Colonel Balogun Sir! What are you….? ", Usman blurted out with some blood from his mouth.

"Never mind what I'm doing, you'll find out soon enough. Right now, we must know, is Jia, Colonel Jia, in the palace?"

Usman replied,

"Yes sir, in his quarters"

"OK what about two of the newest guests of the villa and I don't mean the Libyan or the, 'Palestinian girls' I mean a farmer and the press secretary to the late Lagos Administrator?"

Usman hesitated and Jojo cocked his gun. Usman spoke, turning his eyes to the Colonel,

"Mister, no gun in the world can force me to do what I will not, it is only my respect for Colonel Balogun, knowing that he wouldn't be involved in something he wasn't very convinced of as the right thing! The old man and the journalist are to be executed tonight; they are in this guest house complex upstairs the third floor… ".

Before he finished Desmond had bolted upstairs with four others on his heels.

"How do we do this, should we cut them up piece by piece or strangle them and dispose of their bodies?"

A corporal asked the other with the reply,

"Let us put one in each with muzzle suppressors, we don't want to wake oga from sleep."

The corporal shrugged his shoulders in a surrender to better wisdom. Without any more talk they started to re-assemble their weapons and screwed on their silencers. One of them went ahead to blindfold the two condemned men and gagged them, he was about gagging the second when Desmond burst into the room, the two startled soldiers were slow to respond and died wondering why they and not their captives got shot.

Desmond worked feverishly on the ropes, gagging and blindfolds to loosen them on Chief Kobimdi. When he finished, he fell down on his knees as he stared at the ragged looking figure before him; he was seeing his father for the first time in fifteen years!

Chief Kobimdi was still in shock, barely able to speak or see, he had not the faintest idea his liberator was his son.

Colonel Benjamin Balogun had moved the major to another room under watch and still talking to the major when they heard some noise outside. The door burst open with one of the guest-house attendants rushing in shouting.

"Oga! Oga! Oga! Sir, he - he fell down from stairs… Oga fell down now!"

Ben, Usman, Frank and Emeka followed the man back to one of the palace private reception room where the head of state was having his a private entertainment.

Emeka thought to himself, while observing there were no guards in that section of the building. Clearly, they had confidence that there could be no threat or attack making it to this point without their knowledge, because they met no resistance or any military personnel to challenge or question their presence. As they got to him, Ben instinctively tore off the general's clothing checking for injuries as he tried to resuscitate him. No one noticed that the attendant had slipped away.

"Who the hell are you?!"

It was more of a command then a query.

Ben and company wheeled around to see Colonel Jia the general's CSO with a machine gun pointed at them with other soldiers flanking him.

"Move back!"

"Drop your weapons!"

As they complied, Colonel Jia reached for the general lying on the floor he was foaming in the month but still gasping for breath. Jia dropped his gun and tried to inspect the General's body and the vicinity for signs of what may have transpired. He was about to say something when gunfire shattered the atmosphere and everyone scampered into different directions, some falling in the hail of gunfire, others started shooting back without a clear target all at once.

Six of Jia's men were down, only Jia was left with his chest bleeding from gun shots; Frank too was bleeding from his thigh. The others were still watching from where they had taken cover not sure of what was going on.

Lieutenant Azuka Ubomi stepped cautiously into the room and over to Colonel Jia who was still trying to lift his gun up. Azu stepped on the gun then said,

"This is for making me my own worst enemy Die you bastard, I'll see you in hell!" Emptied the last round of his magazine on Jia's head.

"Ok gentlemen come out now, your baby soldier has come to your rescue!"

When eventually they had all crawled out of their hiding places, they were shocked to see Azu there and he quickly explained how he had put a tracker in his brothers ruck sack and trailed them to the house up till that moment.

Desmond had gathered himself together when Emeka came to get them. They all moved to the guest house where the head of state was. Desmond looked at him questioningly and Michael, reading his mind answered.

"Yes, that was the head of state. He is dead."

"who shot him? What happened?"

Ben spoke.

"We met him choking before his guards came in …."

Desmond noticed the discolored lips and the not so white foam from the general's mouth; sniffed it then looked around and went upstairs. There were three women, bewildered and in a state of shock, it was a sort of bedroom with a water bed in the middle and cushions with other comfort furnishings like a Persian lounge laid out. There had been moved with signs of some kind of playful disturbance and female garments and lingerie littered around. The General was having a one-man party with his girls. He heard the whimpering and turned to face the women. They were more like girls, even in their scared state, tears of terror had washed off most of their make-up and drew ugly looking lines on their faces, he could tell they were not more than nineteen years old – definitely teenagers. They looked middle-eastern on latino, it was a bit hard to tell with all the ugliness on their faces. Two of them were completely nude while the other still had her panties on which looked more like a bunch of stringed beads tied together like G-strings. He couldn't understand how anyone would be comfortable in such a contraption so close to their body let alone sticking into their privates. He still felt G-strings were tools of abuse against women, he tried to speak to the women, but they were either in shock or they didn't understand him. He tried again, only to have the one with G-strings respond in sign language. "Wow!", he thought, sex was really a "shut-up and drive" experience. He tried some Arabic.

"Hal 'ant bikhayr?"

The one closest to him looked up but said nothing. He tried again,

"Hal 'ant bikhayr?"

Louder this time, which startled her and got him a shaky nod in affirmation, then she turned and pointed to the third woman saying.

"Hindiin."

He didn't quite get it until it dawned on him that the third lady was 'Hindi'. Basically, they brought in girls who couldn't understand English so they wouldn't eavesdrop on any local conversation and would do the job they were sent only without unnecessary talk. These girls were skilled in reading body languages of their clients and worked only to give them maximum pleasure and nothing else. No companionship. No presence. Just pleasure slaves, like a fruit platter; you pick when you want and ignore the rest when done. This is what the country's resources were being spent on.

Desmond surveyed the room again and his eye caught on a piece of apple that hadn't more than three bites, the inner surface was pink rather than white or yellow. He understood perfectly well, Ananse must be out of the country by now, the General had been poisoned. it was like table salt; it would be dissolved in water and used to wash the fruit or cup or cutlery anything that would make contact with the inner mouth or tongue. It also had to be carefully mixed to work with only the target's saliva. The idea was for it to trigger either a heart attack or some form of seizure in a person with a pre-existing terminal health or severe condition. It had been mimicked and re-engineered from a similar cocktail used for euthanasia. This made it difficult to tell it wasn't a death by natural cause except you have experience with it already. Such assassins, would leave that singular clue behind that only the initiated could decipher. The arrogance of the expert!

Desmond took the apple and placed it in his pocket; it couldn't harm him even if he ate it.

Emeka joined him

"Yellow we've got trouble, the presidential guards have been alerted, they have surrounded the building. let's get out of here now!"

Desmond followed him down. Frank had his own ideas about having the others go ahead while he gave them cover to escape with Chief Kobimdi and Lance. Colonel Ben had a different idea.

Emeka, Azu, Jojo, Ben, Kukah, Usman and Desmond formed a circle around Osmond and Lance and stepped outside trying to shoot their way through the back to another tunnel.

The guards were already moving into the building as they were finding their way out. They had taken another attendant hostage who guided them through the maze of doors. As they stepped out into the open, they were greeted by a hail of bullets. Fortunately for them that area wasn't as fortified as the front and sides of the building so the resistance was of equal measure.

Bullets were flying, flesh ripping, eyes burning and blood flowing.

Neither the small group of outlaws fighting for their lives nor the presidential guards trying to take back control could have heard the noise of armored tanks rolling towards them and even the thundering of boots, they couldn't have, their attention was on fully in that fire-fight. Additional cover of night made it quite challenging to know who was who. The typical response by a soldier is to keep firing at the direction his mates were shooting. When the return fire dies down, then they can investigate and ask questions. For a typical soldier in a fire fight, as long as you weren't shooting at him or creeping up at him; if you stand or squat or lie next to him shooting in same direction as he is; then no questions asked, you are his ally at that point in time.

Suddenly it was the presidential guards who were cut in a crossfire as they were being shot at. They could hear a bullhorn barking at them to lay down their weapons. It took some more staccato shots before everyone complied and the shooting died down. They could still hear pockets of gunfire but, that was quickly dying out too and replaced by the loudspeaker barking out commands and a few not so amplified voices doing same across the palace grounds and inside.

Desmond and his gang of infiltrators had taken cover beside another building not sure of what was going on. They were still looking for the break to escape.

CHAPTER 6

THE COCK CROWS AT DAWN

It had been one hell of a night.

Colonel Abubakar and Major Chukwudi had received Ben's message which he sent while at the security post. his course mates and friends from Camp Wu Bassey had mobilized their men for the siege. It was the final back-up plan if all else failed. They were to respond to a distress call as the Presidential Guards Brigade. It eventually became their only option.

Ben, had also received news that the potential hotspot key military commands and formations had been normalized and there would be no counter-attack from them. There had been a little problem as two generals who were prominent political figures in the capital and allies to the late general had engaged them in another battle with the remaining loyalist presidential guards from the eastern wing of the palace. Fortunately for them Major General Suleiman had come through for them as well to arrest the situation. He instead relieved the generals of their command and had them put on house arrest.

Terfa and Gerald had brought the pro-democracy people they were holding captive. Ben and Desmond together with Gerald briefed them on the events of that night and told them to discourse the establishment of a new government which would be run by them. They were to vote in one of them as the new president while the rest would double as executive council of advisers and temporary parliament pending a proper election and handover to a democratically elected government. They were not to enact any new laws only to repeal all inhumane and oppressive decrees by the past military juntas to pave the way for freedom and progress. They then left them alone, but not without Desmond warning that if they couldn't sort themselves out, he would!

Desmond went back to the room in the main presidential quarters where they had the late general's family on house arrest. He saw that they were being well treated then he went in to the adjoining room to see his father.

Chief Osmond was sleeping when he came in. Desmond just sat in one corner and stared at him. His clothes had been changed and he suspected, someone may have done it for him and even given him a bath. He wasn't looking as terrible as the first time, but he could still perceive the stench of burnt flesh and bad breath from a mouth that had bled, fed crap and not washed for days on end. His father had been tortured.

Osmond slept for hours and when he woke up, he sat up on the bed and asked Desmond.

"Who are you, who sent you?"

"I am Desmond Kobimdi your son fifteen years ago, your son still today."

Chief, looked around, saw a glass of water and with shaky hands reached for it. Desmond noticed he could barely lift the glass and rushed to help him. As their hands touched, Chief Osmond flinched a little then allowed Desmond to help.

He took a sip, tried to gulp but couldn't swallow, then resigned to gently sipping the water. Desmond spoke softly to him to sip and not gulp the water so it wouldn't hurt him. Chief glanced at him and then closed his eyes briefly and sighed.

"But you are dead, you died fifteen years ago; your mother confirmed it. Not to me though, or am I dead too?"

Anxiety sounding in his voice.

"No papa, that was what mama and I told the world, we too were made to understand you had died until someone saw you in the north. The night we were attacked, mama got to safety but I had to draw the killers away by making them chase me. I escaped thinking that I was the real reason behind the attack, then I got lost and didn't know how to get back so I kept running. I booked a one-way ticket to hell instead of to the US, it's a long story.

My boat was a smugglers' boat, a naval boat patrolling that coast opened fire on us and later another picked my floating body out of the water, they were smugglers and finding I was still alive they rehabilitated me than trained me as one of them. Eventually I got another chance to America. A repentant criminal whose life I had saved adopted me as his son. He processed my immigration papers and I started another life, got an education and became a US Marine, after the USNA Annapolis. I am no longer an active-duty serviceman, now I teach at the University in Texas. Mama and Onyebuchim are with me now and..."

His father interrupted him,

"Who is Onyebuchim?"

"Ah, I'm sorry sir. Papa, Onyebuchim is your daughter; my younger sister, mama gave birth to her November fourteenth that same year, she wants to be a surgeon someday, she's got your fighting spirit and brains. Anyway, we've fared well. Aunty Ketu, wrote me a letter last year that someone saw your ghost coming out of my school compound in the north. So, I hired a private investigator who tracked you down the day you were arrested. Another of my friends was arrested and from then we planned to rescue you. One thing led to another and here we are."

"the head of state is dead and we are coup plotters, the most important thing though, is, you are alive."

He had carefully left out all the clandestine special ops side of his past. How he specialized in counter-insurgency and statecraft - neutralizing situations and criminals under the codename of YELLOW, many thought it meant he was a Japanese.

He also left out the details in his redacted file that his benefactor - Viscount Jean Pierre Nomad had been his target; he was a desperate young man at the mercy of criminals and he was sent to break-in and steal a box. Then he had no idea he was targeting one of the worlds most wanted weapons dealer who wanted to turn himself in as a US Government informer. It turned out that he was being played by the Soviets, even his wife was KGB and the child he thought was his was part of the sham. Unfortunately, those he would bring down thought otherwise.

When he got into the man's house, it was as if the Viscount was expecting him. The man had already slit the throats of his wife and daughter and held the box in his lap just sitting at a desk waiting.

He spoke to Desmond like a child telling him to either take the box and kill him or be killed while attempting to take it but, if Desmond wanted a better life within the law, he should help him escape. He couldn't trust anyone in the immediate area. He knew they had a target on his back.

Desmond was not sure why he chose the Viscount that night, but he did.

The Viscount went underground, had plastic surgery changed his name and other documents, adopted Desmond and together they moved to Colorado.

No one knew what happened to 'Yellow' or the Viscount. 'Yellow' was on the 'Most Wanted List' of Interpol and got some media attention. Some think that like most international hit men, yellow had either been stabbed in one backroom brothel like his predecessors or killed in a hit gone bad or if their suspicions that he is a government agent, then he was hibernating.

The Viscount became a king-maker and died. Desmond ensured he got the private vault he had requested for where his ashes were sealed up with his true birth certificate.

"Hmmmmm, my son you have crossed many bridges and oceans, just like me. I'm sure your mother explained to you that it was actually a battle for the accursed village kingship that my elder half-brother wanted to kill us for? Well after you and your mother fled that night, the fight was bloody, I thought I was dead when I fell, later I woke up in a hospital run by the Catholic Church in Lagos. It was your principal, God rest his soul, late Reverend Father, Thomas Treacy he had received a letter of scholarship for you to study engineering in Massachusetts Institute of Technology, so he drove all the way from Kano down to our house that night, he was the one who took me to the hospital. It was a long time before I healed enough to be aware of my surroundings and sense of what people were saying. I was in a coma for months but they didn't give up on me, they kept nursing and caring for me until I regained consciousness. When I had recovered, your Aunty who had moved out of her house told me you had all died, that was too much for me. My next rehabilitation center was the Yaba Psychiatric hospital. The only visitor I got was Reverend Father Tom. After my discharge, he got me a loan with which I bought a small piece of land, changed my name and started farming, with time my business grew and expanded with the opening of the business center at Apapa. I farmed and traded in the north, exporting and importing other items for my business. I had been trying to get the attention of an American company to invest in my farm, that was my offence that got me here! Never mind what they did to me but, there are many under this building, so what will you do now?" Desmond rubbed his eyes, looked at his watch, it was 03:00 hours, Monday morning.

"Well Papa, the politicians should have solved that for us by now so I can get you out of here and back home!"

He smiled at his father and then walked out of the room.

When he got downstairs his colleagues were eating 'puff-puff' pastries and beverage, he joined them and ate voraciously.

Later went into the room where the civilians were trying to form a government. When he opened the door, there was commotion and they were all talking at once so he had to shout them into silence. He was made to understand there was deadlock since they couldn't agree on one choice for president but they had agreed on other issues like hand over government to a democratically elected executive in nine months, time. Desmond stepped outside for a moment and looked up as he heard slow cautious footsteps in the hallway, he went inside the conference room again then spoke addressing them all.

"I think I have a candidate you cannot but accept!"

After another hour Desmond beckoned all the members of his team including Major General Suleiman and three other generals who had taken sides with them to join the conference.

"Ladies and gentlemen, forgive us for the unconventional and somewhat intrusive style we have used to convey our plans and our intentions. You are all here as members of the first executive council of this new republic which consists of both civilian and military members. This is to be a spring board, a first aid to launch our nation fully into the path of rehabilitation and restoration. We need results, you all know this country better than I do so after careful deliberation by my team and the military high command, we will like you to fashion out a government and a programme that will attend to issues arising, especially political with dispatch as I present to you the interim president of this Federal Republic Mr. Kanayo Osmond Kobimdi!"

Major General Suleiman was made the Vice President and Minister of Defense. At about 10:00 hours that morning, a national broadcast was made introduced by Colonel Abubakar. It started with the usual but unexpected martial music that always sent jitters down the spine of every citizen.

"Fellow countrymen and women, I, Colonel Abubakar D. I., of the Nigerian Army, address you this morning on behalf of the Nigerian Armed Forces and of this Federal Republic. You are all living witnesses to the great economic carnage, predicament and uncertainty, which the past leadership has imposed on our beloved nation for the past couple of years. I am referring to the harsh, intolerable conditions we have all been subjected to living. It has cast a gloom over our polity and society making death, pillage and corruption the order of the day and life expectancy dropping at a fast rate. God in His infinite mercy however, rescued this nation by the sudden death of the previous leader who suffered a heart attack in the late hours of yesterday and since has been buried according to his religious customs. Consequent to this, after due consultations over these deplorable conditions, I and my colleagues in the armed forces and some civilian elder states persons and civil rights activists in the discharge of our roles as promoters and protectors of our national interests have formulated a pathway for this nation to move forward. There has been a change of government, of the Federal Republic. For the first time in our history both the civilian and military populace agreed to act quickly to arrest the wanton destruction of our dear nation under a tyranny, squander-mania, nepotism and corruption that dehumanized us all and made us the laughing stock on the world stage. We have taken certain measures in the best interest of our nation. Very soon the new head of government will deliver his maiden address, note he was voted in by some representatives of the people. Contrary to expectations and as a sign that God did not approve of his tyranny, the former head of state was not killed in a counter coup, he was dead before we got to him, he had a cardiac arrest. He was taken dead…."

He went on to close down the borders and suspend all existing public office holders following the same standard playbook for the weeks following such change in government. There were celebrations on the streets across the country. Even the capitol was not spared, people didn't care they stood in front of soldiers and danced. They tore and defaced pictures of the late ruler, even in some cases soldiers were seen pulling down signposts and posters of him. Then people who had been missing for months, some thought to be dead started to re-appear on the streets. Underground cells in the city; buildings that were secret detention facilities all over the country. There was no one in-charge anymore, so the soldiers who had no reason to keep them just released them and let them go.

EPILOGUE

"Des, we never talked about this, but how many kids would you like us to have?"

Sophia put the question to Desmond,

"Let's see, ten! Mmhnm,"

"What! You must be joking, two only "

Desmond smiled then said,

" Eight, five boys and three girls, "Sophia interjected Mm-mm, four; two boys"

Forgetting about the other guests they were having their own private joke bargaining,

"OK, you've got a deal, shake?"

"No, let's kiss on it."

And he took her lips in his suddenly the hall exploded with applause, then they broke

loose and remembered they were at their own wedding reception. The wedding would have been

a quite well attended one but not even Osmond Kobimdi could stop the media and international

community from showing up and witnesses to the wedding of their ex-president's son who was

well celebrated internationally and locally as the saviour, of the republic. They were called by

the M.C. to have their nuptial dance. Sophia's chief bride's maid took off the tail of her gown so

that she could dance freely, while Desmond handed over his jacket to Michael his best man.

With a fast track playing the newlyweds danced their hearts out for it was their wedding

day. His father had been a man of his words, presided over the interim government for nine

months exactly and handed over to another farmer from the south west of the country.

History would always celebrate his family, they whom were on the verge of extinction

and total annihilation over a miserable village chieftaincy.

God did work in mysterious ways.

His mother and sister had been reunited with their father within days of the announcement. The country had suddenly become a major ally of the US overnight and the State Department easily picked them up and flew them on a US Airforce Hercules escorted by two F-15 fighter jets.

After his father was sworn in, though his sister and himself had returned to Texas, their mother had stayed on after a very emotional reunion; after all her place is with her husband she said.

Konwe and Kingsley went back to school to finish off their exams. The charges against them were dropped and the narrative changed so that Nduka had taken the full blame as being intimidated by cult students over moral issues. All charges were withdrawn and Nduka received a state burial.

On his last night in school, Konwe was packing up his things so he could have an early departure, he didn't want to rush off that night, there were a few parties to attend on campus and he needed the break. An envelope slipped out of his back pack.

It was an envelope that Osa had slipped to him a while back after all the fanfare, he had forgotten about it. He opened it; it was a card with a lovely poem written on it, at the bottom it was signed,

"From mii with love, Osa"

Konwe started laughing then squeezed the card and threw it into the trash. Someone in the room asked him what that was about, a young lady who had an engineering analysis text book on one hand. She was too smart for him, he thought. He answered that it was an old joke, turned round and gave her his full attention.

Osa died the following week.

Konwe's companion was sitting on his study desk, she was wearing wrangler stretch jeans under a purple long sleeved silk blouse with long pointed cuffs and collar. She was very dark skinned and pretty as well as smart; a first-class GPA and a chemical engineering major in her fourth year. True to her bookworm self, she still didn't let go of the textbook; how she was able to have a social life even while solving engineering calculations was a mystery to everyone who knew her. Yet she was a fun person to be with. He smiled at her again and she returned same through her glasses and with their eyes they confirmed to each other – "let's roll".

"Jaiye come on its your treat tonight. Which party are we attending? Yours or mine?"

Konwe locked the door after him and walked down the hall with Jaiye sharing a joke together; he had known but ignored her for over three years, afraid she was out of his league but now she was his girlfriend and they were an item. No hassles, good chemistry.